Tex took a deep breath. "I'm suggesting you marry *me*."

The look on Cissy's face was priceless. Thank God he hadn't had too much invested in the offer, or he'd be devastated. She looked as if she'd just as soon become high priestess of the snake species.

"I don't suppose you want to sleep with me?"

"Now that you mention it—"

"I thought not," she said. "You're a nice guy and cute and smell good and can ride bulls just for the hell of it. But there's marriage, and then there's *marriage,* and when I do it, I really, really want it to be for real."

His Adam's apple jumped in his throat. What could he say? Of course he wanted to sleep with her! But he couldn't say that. Could he?

"We could see what developed," he said hopefully, trying to hedge.

"I know you like trashy girls, Tex," she said, and laid her fingertips against his lips. "And I can be that. If you'll let me."

TEX TIMES TEN
Tina Leonard

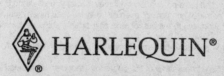

HARLEQUIN®

TORONTO • NEW YORK • LONDON
AMSTERDAM • PARIS • SYDNEY • HAMBURG
STOCKHOLM • ATHENS • TOKYO • MILAN • MADRID
PRAGUE • WARSAW • BUDAPEST • AUCKLAND

I would like to thank Lisa and Dean
for loving their unconventional mother. You are my jewels!

This series happened because of my editors,
Stacy Boyd and Melissa Jeglinski. It's been so much fun! Thanks to you both!

Georgia Haynes,
thank you for reading everything I've ever written—you truly encourage me.
How blessed I've been to have a friend like you!

And to the Scandalous Ladies, who are friends with recipes,
books, stories and so much other great fun that strengthens
and inspires me. I particularly want to thank
Ellen Toomey, Mo Boylan, Tracy Scheetz,
Shawn Schendel, Lynne Thomas, Pam Adamson
and Amy Cunningham.
Thank heavens I became "scandalized"!

ISBN 0-373-16989-2

TEX TIMES TEN

Copyright © 2003 by Tina Leonard.

Visit us at www.eHarlequin.com

Printed in U.S.A.

ABOUT THE AUTHOR

Tina Leonard loves to laugh, which is one of the many reasons she loves writing Harlequin American Romance books. In another lifetime, Tina thought she would be single and an East Coast fashion buyer forever. The unexpected happened when Tina met Tim again after many years—she hadn't seen him since they'd attended school together from first through eighth grade. They married, and now Tina keeps a close eye on her school-age children's friends! Lisa and Dean keep their mother busy with soccer, gymnastics and horseback riding. They are proud of their mom's "kissy books" and eagerly help her any way they can. Tina hopes that readers will enjoy the love of family she writes about in her books. Recently a reviewer wrote, "Leonard has a wonderful sense of the ridiculous," which Tina loved so much she wants it for her epitaph. Right now, however, she's focusing on her wonderful life and writing a lot more romance!

Books by Tina Leonard

HARLEQUIN AMERICAN ROMANCE
748—COWBOY COOTCHIE-COO
758—DADDY'S LITTLE DARLINGS
771—THE MOST ELIGIBLE...DADDY
796—A MATCH MADE IN TEXAS
811—COWBOY BE MINE
829—SURPRISE! SURPRISE!
846—SPECIAL ORDER GROOM
873—HIS ARRANGED MARRIAGE
905—QUADRUPLETS ON THE DOORSTEP*
977—FRISCO JOE'S FIANCÉE†
981—LAREDO'S SASSY SWEETHEART†
986—RANGER'S WILD WOMAN†
989—TEX TIMES TEN†

HARLEQUIN INTRIGUE
576—A MAN OF HONOR

*Maitland Maternity
†Cowboys by the Dozen

THE JEFFERSON BROTHERS
OF MALFUNCTION JUNCTION

Mason (37)—He valiantly keeps the ranch and the family together.

Frisco Joe (36)—Newly married, he lives in Texas wine country with his wife and daughter.

Fannin (35)—Should he pack up and head out to find their long-lost father, Maverick?

Laredo (34), twin to Tex—His one passion: to go east and do Something Big, which meant marrying the love of his life and moving to North Carolina.

Tex (34), twin to Laredo—Determined to prove he's settled, he cross-pollinates roses, but can't seem to get them to bloom.

Calhoun (33)—He's been thinking of hitting the rodeo circuit.

Ranger (32), twin to Archer—He gave up on joining the military to join his wife in their RV.

Archer (32), twin to Ranger—He'll do anything to keep his mind off his brothers' restlessness—even write poetry to his lady pen pal in Australia.

Crockett (30), twin to Navarro—He's an artist who loves to paint portraits—of nudes.

Navarro (30), twin to Crockett—He may join Calhoun in the bull-riding game.

Bandera (26)—He spouts poetry like Whitman—and sometimes nonsense.

Last (25)—Never least, he loves to dispense advice, especially to his brothers.

Prologue

Tex Jefferson's brothers, Frisco Joe, Laredo and Ranger, had tried so hard to outrun a matrimonial state that they'd swerved and crashed headfirst into it.

Tex simply wasn't going to be caught like that. Running was not a fail-safe cure. His brothers had married good women, and they were happy changing their worlds to suit their new wives.

But I, Tex thought, know that marital stability is not my thing. He could ride the orneriest bull. He could bust heads when defense was necessary and sometimes when it wasn't. Rope, ride and range.

But he would die coming home to an Annabelle, a Katy or a Hannah every night. Good girls, every one of them. And Tex was happy for his brothers.

And Mimi Cannady, their next-door neighbor, had put a knot in his eldest brother Mason's life then married someone else. Merry hellfire was Mimi. Tex thought he could almost handle a woman like that.

Maybe. If forced.

But why should he fall for a lady he had no intention of marrying? Mason hadn't married Mimi, and surely that was an example to follow!

But Mason was miserable. Tex was glad to have temporarily left a house that only he and Mason were currently sharing, Tex wandered into one of the riverboat's many bedrooms. He couldn't see himself living on a boat the way Hannah's friend Jellyfish did. Too confining. Too narrow. Louisiana's Mississippi River had its charm but nothing like the great open spaces of Texas and the Union Junction ranch. He was a man of the soil, not a man of the water.

Of course, land was in Tex's blood, as it was in the blood of his eleven brothers: Mason, Frisco Joe, Fannin, Laredo, Calhoun, Ranger, Archer, Crockett, Navarro, Bandera and Last. The men shared three houses on the Union Junction ranch. With Frisco, Laredo and Ranger married, the quarters were getting less crowded, leaving room for Helga the Housekeeper. Tex suspected Mimi had sicced Helga on them to keep Mason ''safe'' from other women—but since Mimi had married Brian, maybe that thought wasn't honorable. Still, Helga had overseen the Jefferson brothers like a strict governess, making the sprawling ranch seem confining.

Startled, he realized he'd stumbled into the newly decorated honeymoon suite—Hannah's bedroom converted for that purpose, as Ranger had mentioned. There were white roses galore and two crystal flutes on the nightstand. Fascinated, Tex ogled the place where love ended up. You met a girl, you married a girl and then you bedded down with the girl, every night for the rest of your life.

Sheesh. Not me, Tex thought.

Next to the crystal flutes was a book that bore Hannah Hotchkiss's name. She was Hannah Jefferson now, since Ranger and she had just said their vows. Through the window, Tex could hear the sound of dance music and happy guests on deck.

He knew he was foregoing dancing for snooping. But he had thought Cissy Kisserton might make it to Hannah's wedding, since the two of them had gotten close during their infamous road trip with Ranger. He'd hoped for a glimpse of that platinum-haired man-magnet; a glimpse was about all a man could handle. But she hadn't attended.

Being nosy, Tex picked up Hannah's book. A picture fell to the floor, which he scooped up guiltily.

And there was Cissy Kisserton, looking like no Cissy he'd ever seen. She wasn't dressed in a miniskirt and high heels. She wasn't wreaking havoc on a man's groin by wearing catsuit jeans.

This Cissy was dressed for church.

Whew. She was a wicked brew of sin underneath that churchy lace thing. Who was she trying to fool?

Tex wasn't admitting it, but he'd stayed on that bull, BadAss Blue, just to impress Cissy. Sure, she'd lied about the other bull, Bloodthirsty, pulling left so that Tex's twin, Laredo, wouldn't be able to stay on.

But Tex sort of admired a woman with gall.

And he'd stayed on his bull just to show Cissy Kisserton what he was made of. He figured she'd be appropriately admiring and grateful after the rodeo.

She hadn't been.

It was as if she had too many things on her mind

to be bothered with him. A winning cowboy, and she hadn't given him the time of day. He'd beat his own brother—not that it was difficult since Laredo couldn't have stayed on a bull if he'd had crazy glue in his jeans—just to get *her* attention.

Tex turned his gaze back to the picture. Seven children stood around Cissy, some of them clinging to her. There was a church in the background. In fact, she was standing in a church parking lot. The baby stroller at her side held what looked like two more infants, and, he saw with a growing sort of horror, her left hand was on the stroller handle!

Tex's jaw sagged as if he'd been punched in a bar brawl. The nine little moppets of varying ages were going to church with *her*.

Chapter One

If I knew everything, I'd be less of a man
Maverick Jefferson to his sons when they
bragged to Mimi that their father knew more
than Mimi's father, Sheriff Cannady

"Wimmin are tricky," Tex Jefferson stated, his
voice slurring. "I think they aim to trick ush poor
men into matrimony and sex and giving money at
church and even stealing candy from babies. Don-
choo think?"

Newlyweds Hannah and Ranger Jefferson stared
down at Ranger's thirty-four-year-old brother, who
was lolling in the middle of their unchristened honeymoon bed. Tex had obviously helped himself liberally to wedding champagne.

"Tex, dude, that's all fine and good, but you're
going to have to vacate. What are you doing in here,
anyway?" Ranger asked.

"Hidin' from wimmin," Tex told them, trying to
roll onto his side to achieve an upright position and
failing miserably as he listed to the left, back onto

the down pillows. "Did you notice all the wimmin out there at the reception? They're plotting," he said to Ranger in a hushed whisper. "I could tell they were plotting something. It's not safe!"

Ranger cleared his throat. "I don't think it's you they're after, particularly. Here, let me heave your arse out of our bed. Hannah and I have a wedding night to enjoy, without you, bro."

Together, Hannah and Ranger pulled Tex to his feet and helped him—pushed him—to the door.

Tex peered owlishly down the hall. "Are they gone?"

"Who?" Hannah asked.

"The wimmin!"

"Yes," she said. "Now, you head on to bed. You'll be safe in your own room."

"Okay. 'Night," Tex said, lurching down the hall. He wasn't certain if this riverboat suited him or not. It was pretty and all. He felt claustrophobic. Or maybe he felt left out. He certainly hadn't wanted to dance with Hannah's stylist sisters from the Lonely Hearts salon. That way led to certain danger. And he hadn't wanted to stand around and gab with his brothers—all they did anymore was rib him about his problems with his rose beds. Budus Interruptus! Shoot, it was only April! Who expected a rose to open in April, anyway? All right, so tomorrow began the month of May, but it was his opinion that anything that took a long time was worth waiting for. When they finally bloomed, his roses were going to be so spectacular his brothers would shut up for good.

He hoped.

He'd endured a lot of ribbing about those roses, and his own "unplowed" field. Only at Malfunction Junction would a man's lack of a sex life be such a game topic of conversation. His eleven brothers: all lures to the female gender. And he, Tex, lately eschewing female companionship. For two months now, though he wasn't counting.

But his brothers were.

"Mind their own beeswaxes," he said to himself, opening the door to his room. "I don't need any wimmin. Nothing but trouble. Arrgh!" he cried, his brain late to assess what his eyes were surveying in disbelief. The entire female wedding party was assembled in his room.

Maybe it wasn't his room. He backed up and looked at the letter on the door, but one of the girls took his hand and pulled him inside, closing the door behind him.

"Hello, Tex," they chorused.

It was a she-wolf pack. A curse. He was going down. They were after him, and he didn't know a man who could outrun more than a dozen determined females.

He was vastly outnumbered.

"Can I have a last meal?" he asked.

CISSY KISSERTON GLANCED over the Never Lonely Cut-n-Gurls salon, counting the number of male cus-

tomers for her report to Marvella. In the past couple
of weeks, Cissy had become resigned to her fate—
one more year serving as Marvella's hostess. She
wished she'd known about the salon's brothel reputation, but a girl did what she had to do, especially
when she had nine mouths to feed.

With a glance around, she slipped upstairs to call
her grandmother, who cared for the children her siblings and their spouses had left behind when they'd
become missionaries and found themselves in a hot-
bed of rebel activity. The Lord giveth, and the Lord
taketh away. He'd taken, and she still didn't know if
her siblings were dead or alive.

"Gran?" Cissy said when the phone was answered.

"Hey, honey," her grandmother said.

A small smile touched Cissy's face as the memory
of oatmeal-raisin cookies and homemade soups
flowed over her. The warmth of her grandmother's
home. A blooming garden outside where the sun
kissed the earth, even in winter. "How are the kids?"
Cissy asked.

"How are you?" Gran countered.

"I'm fine."

"You don't sound fine. You sound sad."

Cissy drew a deep breath. "Just a little homesick,
is all."

"I know. I can tell. How 'bout I send you a box
of your favorite cookies?"

"Tell me how the baby is doing? And the other
children? And you?" Cissy said, battling back tears.

"We're fine and dandy. I took your last check and went out and bought the kids new crayons. And some shorts from the secondhand store for the bigger ones. You won't believe how much these young'uns have grown."

"I know I wouldn't." Cissy sat down on the bed and picked at the comforter.

"Well, we all miss you, but you shouldn't be spending your money on calling us so often. Sunday nights are fine. Besides, the children are all in bed now. You've missed speaking to them."

Cissy shook her head. "I really just wanted to hear your voice. I'm feeling much better now."

"Cissy," Gran said, "there's just no way out of that contract with Marvella, is there?"

"No." Although for a few days last month, Cissy had hoped and prayed that she'd escaped with Hannah Hotchkiss's help. Tonight, her friend would become Hannah Jefferson. And Cissy couldn't go to the wedding because she had to work. An iron-clad contract with Marvella and a desperate need for money to send to her family was enough to make certain Cissy stayed exactly where she was. "It's good money, Gran. I'm glad you bought the kids new crayons. They couldn't have a better teacher than you."

And that was the truth. If there was a happy place to grow up, it was Gran's. "I have to go now," she said softly. "Tell the children I'll call on Sunday."

"You do that. And Cissy," her grandmother said,

"there's a light at the end of this tunnel. We just haven't seen it yet."

"I'm sure it's there."

"Clearly, I'm going to have to dream up a hand-some-prince-rescues-my-Cissy scenario for you. I just don't know any handsome princes."

"I don't know any that provide rescue service. Good night, Gran. I love you."

"I love you, too."

She hung up the phone, feeling better and worse all at once. Lost in thought, she was startled when the phone rang under her hand. "Hello?"

"Shishy?" a voice said.

Cissy frowned. "This is Cissy."

"Thish ish Tex."

"Tex…Jefferson?"

"Uh-huh."

"You sound…like you've enjoyed the wedding." Her heart began pounding. Why would that hand-some cowboy be calling her? It was as if her dreams were coming true…but of course, the dreams she dreamed couldn't possibly come true for her.

"I haven't enjoyed anything!" he said urgently, though his voice was hushed.

"What is your problem?" she demanded. "You sound like you're in a pipe."

"I'm not in a pipe! I'm in a jam. I need you to save me!"

Her brows shot up. "Oh, gosh, thank heaven. There for a minute I thought my Prince Charming might actually be calling me."

"What?"

"Nothing. Saving cowboys isn't exactly my specialty. And besides, it sounds like you're about three bottles past salvation."

"These wimmin want me. That's the problem!"

She laughed. "Tex, that's a male oxymoron."

"Oxy-what? I'm not in the mood for big chat, Cissy. I need you to come get me out of here before they find me!"

"Where are you?"

"In a broom closet on the riverboat!"

She sat on the bed, beginning to enjoy his dilemma. "Hiding from women."

"Yes!"

"Pawn them off on your brothers. How was the wedding?"

"I dunno. I fell asleep."

"And then you found the champagne."

"Well, yes. And then they grabbed me. And so I found more champagne. But it's starting to taste sharp to me. I need a good old-fashioned beer."

"Who grabbed you?"

"The women from the other two salons."

Oh. Her rivals. Hannah's stylist sisters. "Most men don't complain about women wanting them, Tex. Is there a problem you want to share?"

"No," he said, his voice tense. "It's what they want to do with me that's the problem."

"And that would be?"

"Raffle me. And my brothers. My brothers are going to kill me, because I agreed. But there was just so much pressure, Cissy!''

He was starting to sound better now that he was putting voice to his anxiety. Cissy crawled up in her bed and leaned against the headboard. ''What kind of pressure?'' Although she could imagine, since he was a gorgeous guy.

''I don't know. Pressure!''

''I have to take a report to Marvella, Tex. You go sleep off your pressure, okay? I think you'll be fine in the morning.'' She should have known that the only reason he'd ever ring her phone was if he was three sheets to the wind and heading downstream fast.

''Cissy, listen to me. This is really all your fault.''

''Mine?''

''Yes. Because you told my brother that Bloodthirsty Black pulled left, when he didn't. Laredo could have been killed!''

''He could have been killed, anyway, since he couldn't ride a bull. How is that my fault?''

''Because you work for the wicked witch. And Hannah suggested a cowboy raffle to get you out of your contract. Only Marvella turned down the idea, and now the other salons have picked it up. And I got roped into taking part.''

''You wouldn't want to be on this salon's team, Tex. It's definitely not the team of good sportswomanship.''

''I know. And what will happen if I get won? Have you ever considered that, Miss Kisserton?''

"Oh," she said. "You're figuring that someone in this salon might buy you."

"Marvella," he said, sounding squeaky. "I mean, what if?"

She laughed. "I don't think she wants you, cowboy."

"She might. To ride BadAss Blue for her. Or some other enslavement. Think, Cissy. I could end up dancing on her hot tub wearing nothing more than a pair of jeans! Or she might make me be a butler for an evening, her personal boy-toy."

"The possibilities are endless," Cissy said. "But I think you're overrating your appeal." Actually, he wasn't, but Cissy wasn't going to reward his vanity or his paranoia.

A knock on her door made her jump. "Who is it?"

"Marvella."

"Hang on," she whispered to Tex. "Marvella wants to talk to me. Come in," she called.

Her nemesis walked in, dressed in a conservative navy-blue dress, her white hair piled high and iron-sprayed. "I've been waiting for the report." She eyed Cissy's clothing with approval, and then the phone Cissy was holding with disapproval.

"I'm sorry. I got an unexpected phone call. Fifty customers downstairs, including the mayor and a police captain from the town over. Drink tab is up by fifty percent. And the cowgirl-loving ship captain is back, paying court to Valentine. He likes her phone-voice so much he hasn't yet figured out she can't ride a horse.''

"Good." Marvella nodded. "Who are you talking to?"

Cissy swallowed. "Tex Jefferson."

"Excellent." Her voice turned soft and cooing. "Please tell Tex I say hello. And that I'm so hoping he'll ride BadAss Blue for me at this month's Mayfest. I'm also thinking of doing a children's petting zoo, if he can think of some animals I could rent for the event."

Cissy's jaw went slack. "I told you," Tex said in her ear. "She'll think of a way to use and abuse me!"

"I'll tell him, Marvella," Cissy said.

Marvella smiled. "Good night."

"Good night." She waited until Marvella closed the door. "Now, don't get all wadded up," she told Tex.

"Oh, no, I have no reason to be wadded. But this is your fault."

She gasped. "Nothing is my fault!"

"You told Laredo that Bloodthirsty cranked left, which caused me to have to get involved, and now Marvella wants me. And if she gets the chance to win me, I'm toast."

"You have toast between your ears. It's simply not as bad as you paint it. So you'll ride a bull. That's not exactly a stretch for you."

"But I don't want to ride for Marvella anymore," Tex said. "It hurts Delilah's feelings. She doesn't say so, but I feel uneasy. And I've learned to pay attention to my uneasy feelings.''

Delilah owned the salon across the street, and the two sisters stayed at each other's throats. Marvella accused Delilah of stealing Marvella's husband many years ago, but Cissy privately thought Marvella's meanness had probably run her husband off. ''I think Delilah understands the situation.''

''I'm not going to do it,'' Tex said suddenly. ''I refuse to take part in this charity event.''

''Have it your way. It's no big loss, I'm sure. I have to go,'' she told him. ''Thanks for calling. I think.'' Actually, she was a little miffed that he'd only called to cry on her shoulder.

She wanted him to call her because he wanted to talk to her. Really talk to her. Not just wheeze. Even though she felt like wheezing about Marvella herself.

''Okay. I just needed to hear you say that ducking out on a charity event was all right.''

''It's fine. You have given yourself permission to be a weasel. Good night.'' And she hung up the phone.

But five hours later, when Cissy was sound asleep in her bed, something sat on her feet. Something large. She let out a shriek and struggled to sit up.

''Sh,'' the something large said. ''It's Tex.''

''What are you doing?'' she demanded furiously, though she was greatly relieved to know it was Tex and not a patron of Marvella's. ''How did you get into my room?''

"We'll discuss terms of entry later," he said. "Right now, I've got to talk to you."

She switched on her side-table lamp, tucking in a startled breath when she got a look at the gorgeous man sitting on her feet. Hot enough to radiate his own heat. And yet, she didn't dare melt for him again. "Could you get off of me?" she asked.

He didn't move. Instead, he handed her a white box. "Wedding cake. Hannah commissioned me to courier this to you. Actually, she also told me the secret to getting into Rapunzel's ivory tower. Of course she wasn't expecting me to drop in on you in your sleep, but I prefer the thrill of surprise." He handed her some wedding napkins that had Ranger's and Hannah's names entwined in burgundy, and a rose he'd swiped from the table decorations. "Now, this is a rose," he said. "This I envy. But I give it to you. And I'll stop with the brownnosing there."

"Oh," Cissy said, taking the box and the rose and trying to ignore the fact that she was slightly mollified. "Thank you. I mean, tell Hannah I said thank you, although not for telling you how to breach the tower," she said, regaining the stiffness in her voice just to let him know he was not forgiven for breaking in. She allowed her gaze to run swiftly over him, drinking him in though she faked disinterest. "Now, could you get off me?"

Tex stared at her, his eyes dark in the lamplight. Her heart began pounding. If she didn't know better, she'd think that was lust burning in his gaze.

"Here." She thrust the cake box at him. "Please put that on my dresser over there."

The second he got up to do it, Cissy leaped out of the bed and grabbed her robe, tossing it on and tying it tight. "I should scream for security." She frowned as she put the rose in a silver vase that sat on her dresser.

"Do you ever plan on telling Marvella that you're married?" Tex asked after a long perusal of her silvery satin bathrobe. "Not that it matters or anything, in the overall scenario, but I wondered if you ever planned on telling anyone the truth, besides Hannah."

"Whose business is it?" Cissy crossed her arms.

"Well, that's the funny thing," Tex said, pushing back his cowboy hat as he stared down at her. "I've decided to make it mine, Mrs. Kisserton."

Chapter Two

"Well, that's the even funnier thing," Cissy said, fixing a gaze on Tex that seemed angry and amused all at once. God, he loved a woman with attitude. "I got a phone call today from the chief of police in our small town. My husband was sort of...located."

Tex's heart slid south. Maybe he'd quit breathing.

Then he told himself to buck up and focus. What did he care that some loser of Cissy's was still around? "Yeah? So where's he been?"

She pursed her lips at him in a thoughtful expression, and he had to admit the expression made him thoughtful, too.

"He's been in a lake, wearing specially fitted diving gear."

Tex frowned, and Cissy sighed. "He'd been tossed in with chains. Apparently, he'd been shot first, and then the culprits weighted his body so it wouldn't be found. And not much of it was, I guess. Nothing identifiable without multiple lab tests, anyway."

"I'm sorry." His arms hung at his side, feeling useless as oak trees. "Can I do something for you?"

"Like maybe call before you drop in?" Cissy asked. "I generally prefer to have advance notice from visitors."

He scratched his neck. "Not to be heavy-handed, but you don't seem all that broken up about being widowed."

She stared at him. "Tex, my marriage was unusual. It was a marriage of convenience for both of us. I would be a politically appealing wife, and he'd take care of my three younger siblings and their children, and me, and Gran. But that's not exactly how it all worked out, obviously, or I wouldn't have signed a contract with Marvella. When I came to Lonely Hearts Station, I hadn't seen him in two years." Her whole demeanor said, That's my story—I don't care if you like it or not. "The money is good, and my family eats."

He couldn't believe his ears. "Your marriage wasn't real?"

She raised her brows at him. "As real as anyone else's. Oh, you're asking the indelicate question."

He could feel his neck turn red, but yeah, he was all for asking indelicate questions if she'd answer them. Curiosity and burning hope lay deep in his heart. Maybe she hadn't loved the guy. Maybe she wasn't in true mourning, which would require him to give her breathing space, for a long time, to put her marriage and her feelings about her husband—

Whoa, Nelly. He stopped his thoughts with a hard jerk. "No," he said, his voice hard, "I'm not asking any indelicate questions."

"Really? Because I could have sworn you were—"

"Well, I wasn't." But he had been.

Once Hannah had slipped and mentioned that Cissy was married, he'd had to know why Cissy had made love with him in the barn two months ago, an experience he couldn't get out of his head. It was so unlike him—and his brothers would be amazed if they suspected. "It's none of my business. Why would I care?"

They stared at each other, belligerence on both their faces. Then Cissy broke eye contact and went to the box he'd brought, lifting the top so she could see inside. "So, did you slither under the door?"

He didn't bother to answer. Lamplight from the side table backlit her, and he could make out curves under the robe and gown. Not that he hadn't seen plenty of Cissy's curves. Anyone who looked at her got an eyeful. Slippery and graceful under the icy satin, those curves made his throat dry out and his heart jump in his chest. A part of his body south of his heart jumped, too, staying in an arrested position, like a freeze-frame of a basketball player going to the hoop.

She stuck a finger into the icing and put it in her mouth, turning to see why he wasn't answering her question and immediately guessed his thoughts.

He expected her to flush, but she didn't. She just acted as if she didn't care.

Which he found vaguely disappointing.

"Back to slithering," she said.

"I won't tell you how I got in, but it wasn't difficult." Not nearly as difficult as trying to figure out what it was exactly that he felt for Cissy. Obviously, he hadn't expected to have the urge to toss her in bed and take her as if there was never going to be a tomorrow.

"Oh, come on. Tell me. If you do, I'll be sure to double-block that entrance," she said, her tone wheedling, as if she were offering him something he wanted.

She knew very well he wasn't going to tell her. "Should I say I'm sorry about your husband?" he asked. "Pretend that I have good manners?"

Her aquamarine eyes settled on him. "Are you sorry?"

"Yeah. I get the feeling you've been through enough."

With a sigh, she tucked a strand of silvery hair behind her ear. "I'm just Miss Kisserton. That's my maiden name. I didn't use my husband's name after I came to work for Marvella. I didn't want any reminders of what kind of life he was living. According to the police, it was high-dollar drugs and glamorous parties. Parties at which I was often the unsuspecting hostess. Believe me, my skin creeps when I think about my own part in what was going on." She looked at him sadly. "I should have guessed, but I was so busy concentrating on being the perfect wife and hostess that I didn't pay attention to what now seems obvious."

He waited, realizing she wanted to talk.

"I feel very guilty about that," she murmured. "I wish I'd known. I'd never have married him."

"It's not your fault."

"I tell myself that." She replaced the lid and went to sit on the bed. "But it doesn't help."

With her guard down, Cissy looked like a young girl. Innocent, fragile and beautiful. The combination packed a powerful punch.

She looked up at him. "I learned my lesson about rescues. There's no such thing as a handsome prince."

"I believe you," he agreed. "I think there's no such thing as a handsome princess."

She laughed at him. "Do you need rescuing?"

"Nah. Occasionally my brothers get on my nerves, but I can handle them." He tore his gaze away from her, telling himself that it would be easy to put the strange, unexpected feelings he was experiencing back inside their long-forgotten hiding place. "And I wouldn't like a princessy kind of girl, anyway. I like trashy girls."

Her eyes rolled. "There are plenty on the premises. I'd be happy to find you one to talk to—"

"No, no," he said hastily. "It's after hours and you're off duty as a hostess. I'd better go."

She nodded at him. "All right."

He tipped his hat to her.

"I'm very curious to see how you do this," she said.

"Do what?"

"Leave. Since I have no idea how you got in."

"Oh." He grinned. "Okay."

He unlocked her door, opened it and left.

She jumped off the bed and jerked the door open, pulling him back inside.

"A simple 'please stay' is sufficient," Tex said.

"You can't let anyone see you!" Cissy said. Then she paused. "Do you want to? Stay?"

"Do dogs have ears?" he demanded.

She locked the door behind him. "I noticed that you were attracted to me, but I felt that was probably your standard reaction to any female in a bathrobe."

"Very likely," he agreed, not missing the chance, while they were close, to smell her. Honeysuckle. "You don't smell like a bad girl."

Her eyes widened. "Strange. You smell like a bad boy."

"And how is that?"

She sniffed him as they stood against the door. "Leather. Aftershave. A beer or two. And…something I can't quite name."

Leaning close, she smelled his neck. Her hair feathered against his collarbone and under his chin, and his erection returned full force.

"Sex?" she asked, her eyes wide.

"Don't mind if I do," he replied, sweeping her playfully into his arms.

"No," she said, pushing against his chest until she freed herself. "I think you smell sexy. Maybe *manly* is the word I'm searching for."

"I hope that's a good thing," he said, taking her

hand and kissing it. "If not, we could take a shower together."

She wrinkled her nose and pulled her hand away. "I don't think so. Something tells me water conservation with you would be detrimental to my health."

For the moment, he forbore further wisecracking, since he was definitely experiencing resistance from her. He decided not to take it personally, considering they were two birds of a feather, and he felt like resisting her, too. "Okay, if I can't leave the way I came in, how do you expect me to go?"

"I don't know." She watched him as he snagged the cake box and sat on her bed. "What are you doing?"

"Eating your un-wedding cake." He lifted the lid and pulled out a hunting knife from his jacket pocket.

She gasped. He glanced up.

"Overkill, I know. But would you rather I use my fingers?" He cut a neat slice from the cake.

A second later, she joined him on the bed. "You might as well cut me a piece, too. It doesn't look as if you're leaving anytime soon."

"Oh, I'm leaving, all right. I just need a sugar boost before I jump out your window. I'm not a superhero, you know."

He felt her stare at him in amazement, and he decided he liked having her attention on him like that.

"Can you jump out a second-story window in your condition?" she asked.

He hesitated in the act of handing her a slice of

cake. "What condition? I'm in prime physical shape."

"Well—" She gestured toward his crotch, which was still distended from their close call by the door. When she'd drawn near to smell him, he'd definitely felt the impact.

"Oh, that," he said nonchalantly. "Don't you worry about that. Sugar boost'll take care of that in a flash."

"Really?"

"Sure." He bit into the cake. "Eat your un-wedding cake."

"What is un-wedding cake, anyway?"

"Well, if you learned today that you're no longer married, I suppose that's what this should be. We can be sad if you want to be, though," he offered hastily.

"Oh, no. Please. I wouldn't think of it." She tasted her cake, too. "I'm just glad to know that he was finally found. I wouldn't have felt right remarrying if I'd never learned what happened to him. I have no idea what the marital expiration date is on husbands who disappear. It could be a decade, for all I know."

"Hey, this is un-wedding cake. Do not sleep with this under your pillow and try to dream of your future husband. Old wives' tales don't really work," he said sternly.

"I'll probably never get married again, anyway," she said, finishing off her cake. "I've got too many kids to care for."

"And that's something I've been meaning to ask you," he said, cutting another piece for himself. "How many children do you have? Because I found a picture of you in Hannah's room, and I think I counted nine. Nine!" He looked at her, his heart in his throat. "Those weren't your responsibilities, were they?"

She looked at him for a long time, and he didn't like the depth of her gaze. It told him all he needed to know, and he didn't need the lie of a sugar boost to ease the strain in his jeans. His pants started fitting better instantly.

"They're all mine—nephews and nieces," she said. "There are ten of us. If one doesn't count Gran. And then there are my missing three siblings, which, if and when they ever come back into the picture, will make fourteen."

"You support fourteen people."

"Well, my brother and sisters are missionaries. They're gone a lot, and they don't make much. Gran used to be able to work, but now that she's older, she gets tired more easily."

"Taking care of nine kids would tire me out."

"Yes, but we didn't expect my family to be gone so long. They left for a weekend to take coats and blankets to a sister church in South America."

To his dismay, her eyes filled with the first tears he'd ever seen her cry. "Wait, wait," he said. "Don't do that. They'll be back, I'm sure."

"I'm not so certain anymore." She got up to wash her hands and dry her eyes at the washstand sink in her room. "We haven't heard from them in almost three years. The government won't tell us anything. And needless to say, Gran and I do not have enough money to hire an investigator."

And then he saw her shoulders shaking. Oh, boy. Putting the cake back into the box, he moved it back to the dresser. "Cissy," he murmured, going to stand behind her. "You've got a great ass."

"What?"

She turned to stare at him, and he prepared to dodge a slap. "It was all I could think of to make you stop crying," he admitted. "I don't have much experience with women's tears."

She put her hands on her hips. "I wasn't crying."

Now who was fibbing? And yet, he understood covering up. "My brothers say I have an intimacy problem," he offered.

Her eyes widened. "No man admits to something like that."

"I didn't say I had one. That's what they like to accuse me of. It's not true."

"Is that why you're here?"

He frowned at her. There was a real reason he was there—to deliver the cake as Hannah had requested. And then there was the real-real, albeit inadmissible, reason he was there—to see Cissy. But neither of those reasons could be what Cissy had in mind. "What?"

"Because of your intimacy problem."

"Why would I come here for that? Just saying I had one, which I don't."

"Because this salon is the place men like to come to lose their *intimacy* problems. And a whole host of other problems."

His jaw sagged. "You're suggesting that I—"

"Not suggesting. Asking, cowboy. Asking."

No. The answer was no.

And yet, he had to admit he was pulled to Cissy in a sort of strange, like-what-I-see-but-can't-touch-it way. It was a sexual paradox of sorts.

Which would play into his brothers' theory.

"I've always espoused the 'don't ask, don't tell' policy of life," he said.

"And yet you've asked plenty of questions about my life. My family."

"Yeah. That's when I thought you were my kind of girl."

She stared at him. "And now you think I'm...?"

He shifted uncomfortably. "I guess you're a good girl. A good girl with issues, but I definitely see why Hannah likes you."

"And so that crosses me off your short list."

"I don't have a list," he replied.

"But if I were a wild woman, I'd be on it."

"Well, that, and if you wore interesting lingerie. I'm going to develop a fetish for interesting lingerie."

She sighed. "Tex, I think you have an intimacy problem."

He sighed, too, and laid back across the bed horizontally. She lay next to him, and they both stared lackadaisically at the ceiling, their legs hanging off the bed. "Not if I have a fetish."

"You don't, cowboy. You said you're going to develop one. Like, maybe when you're forty? Not that any of this matters, since I'm not your kind of girl or anything."

"And thank heavens for that," he said. "I do not want to end up like my brothers. Even though they're happy," he said expansively, "that is no reason to emulate them."

"Back to the raffle," she reminded him. "I think you should do it."

"Why?"

"It would prove to your brothers that you don't have any issues," she pointed out. "You would also prove it to yourself, because on a subconscious level, you could be in denial." She beamed at her attempt at psychoanalysis. "And it's for a good cause."

They turned their heads to look at each other. It was, Tex realized at that moment, too close for comfort. "You may not be a trashy girl," he said, "but you didn't slap me when I said you had a great ass."

"That's because I felt sorry for you," she said softly, staring into his eyes. "I knew there had to be a reason you were trying so hard to be something you weren't."

He could practically feel his eyes bug from their sockets. "Now comes the enlightenment. What am I not?"

"A badass cowboy."

"So you're figuring I'm a pansy."

"You're neither. Just right down the middle. A nice guy."

Just what he'd always wanted. "Maybe you're not as smart as you think you are."

She shrugged, a little icily for his taste, especially since she was lying on her back and shouldn't have been able to get that much movement into a shrug.

"Okay. Let me ask you something. If I was a trashy girl—your favorite kind—would you have tried to hit on me by now? I mean, you're holding back for some reason. In fact, you're almost a hypocrite. You tease about kissing me and having sex and say I've got a great behind, and it's clear you like what you see, but then you treat me like a sister."

"I don't have sex on the first date," he said gruffly.

"You did," she reminded him. "If meeting me in a barn can be called a date."

"It can't," he argued. "That was a first meeting, and I'd definitely never done that before." He moved his head back to stare at the ceiling. "There are moral imperatives involved."

She rolled up on her elbow and looked at him quizzically. "Are you quoting someone?"

"No," he said, not about to admit that some of his brother Bandera's philosophical ditherings and their father's teachings had soaked into his skull. "I'm only trying to illustrate that I'm not a loser or an intimacy-phobe. I don't have to mate like a gorilla."

"Now that you've decided that I'm not a trashy girl."

Truly, the woman had superior insight. He couldn't have had sex with her if he wanted to now. Really. She was no different than Annabelle, Katy or Hannah—and look where those girls had led his unsuspecting brothers! "I don't have to prove anything to my brothers. Or myself. I'll do the raffle because charity is a good thing."

"I see."

Tex's brows rose. He heard the snarkiness in her tone. Okay, maybe *disbelief* was more the word. "All right," he said. "That's it. Even a gentleman can only take so much—and I'm not even a gentleman. So I'm way past my limit, lady."

And then he pinned her beneath him.

Chapter Three

Cissy held her breath as the cowboy on top of her lay still. They stared into each other's eyes as if they had never seen each other before. Cissy's heart beat slowly, yet very hard, in her throat. "Well, cowboy," she said, "as you said, this is it."

"Now or never."

"Do or die," she said, loving the feel of Tex's weight on her. "Here we are, again."

And yet he remained frozen.

"I promise I don't bite on the first real kiss," she teased.

"I do," Tex said, touching his lips briefly to hers. "You taste like un-wedding cake."

"Is that a good thing?"

"It's maybe the best cake I ever had," he said, lowering his head so that he could kiss her, and taste her more deeply. She moaned, arching, wanting to be tighter against him as she ran her hands up over his back.

Before she knew what was happening, he pulled

away. Her heart plummeted as he got off the bed. "What happened?" she asked.

"Nothing," he said. *Everything.*

"Did your escape hatch fly open?" she demanded, sitting up on the bed to glare at him.

Tex didn't like the sound of that. "Meaning?"

"No man leaps away from a woman like his pants are on fire, when a moment before he was sucking at her lips like a drowning man sucks air. Maybe your intimacy issue returned full force."

He bit the inside of his jaw. His pants were definitely on fire, but he shifted so she couldn't notice. "I'm trying to be a gentleman. I don't want to take advantage of you."

"Oh, please. You think that if you kiss me and like it too much—maybe even make love to me again—you'll end up at the altar like your brothers. You don't want to fall in love. Which is perfect as far as I'm concerned, because I'm the last girl who wants to see a wedding ring."

There went that unattractive prescient side of her. "I could kiss you all day and not fall in love," he lied, his pride in full force. "Heck, I could kiss twenty girls and not fall in love! Marriage is not a good way for men to live. All that devotion and fidelity stuff is hard on a guy."

"Guess you won't have any trouble with that raffle, after all," Cissy said.

He didn't like the gleeful smile on her face. "Sounds like the most fun I'll have all year."

"I'll have to come watch."

That hadn't entered his thoughts, and he wasn't certain he was entirely comfortable with Cissy watching women bid on him. "Uh—"

"I could be a mole bidder and drive up your price," she offered.

Did he hear revenge in her tone? "A mole bidder?"

"You know, every time someone bids, I outbid them, so that they have to bid again. Of course, I have no intention of buying you."

Trying to ignore her obvious disinterest in him—where was the jealousy, for heaven's sake?—Tex puffed out his chest. "How much do you figure I'm worth?"

"Ten, twenty bucks?"

His brows shot to his hairline. "Oh, come on. Be real. I've still got all my teeth!"

"Well, that does count for something," she said reluctantly. "How's your continence?"

"My what?"

"You know. Your…you know." She gestured to his jeans.

"Oh, my continence!" he exclaimed. "I can go all night."

"You don't say." Her gaze swept his jeans and then lingered a moment more. "And you've got a full head of hair," she said. "I think you'll fetch about fifty bucks. I'd bid on you," she said with a sigh, "but I'm financially embarrassed these days, and Lord only knows I wouldn't know what to do with you if I won you. I suppose I could put you to work in the rose garden out back. I know how much roses appeal to you, those secretive buds of romance.''

Though he knew she was tweaking him, it was getting on his nerves. He'd just kissed her. Darn it, she should be acting more…more, well, appreciative. And interested. After all, he didn't go around kissing just any girl. In fact, he hadn't kissed anybody in a long time. Nobody since her.

Maybe that was his problem. He was out of practice. He was taking it all too seriously. ''I need a trashy girl to purchase me,'' he said.

''Oh, yes, the only type for you.''

''Well, there're reasons for that.''

She frowned at him. ''Thanks for bringing me the cake, Tex. If you don't mind, I think I'll go to sleep now. I've got to work tomorrow.''

He nodded, noting the distance in her tone. ''All right, Cissy. I'll tell Hannah you're doing fine.''

''You do that,'' she said absently, turning away.

And darn it, she didn't even seem to notice when he raised the window. Glancing at her, he realized her thoughts were somewhere else. She'd pulled some pictures from a drawer in her nightstand, but he couldn't see what they were. Caught between bravado and bragging, he decided there was no other way to get her attention back on him.

He jumped.

Then he waited for her to look out to make certain he was in good health, his head crooked around so that he could see her expression.

She closed the window. The lace drapes fell together.

"Damn," he said to himself, limping toward his truck. "Even superheroes get a little applause for exiting out of windows!"

But Cissy hadn't seemed to care, much like she hadn't seemed impressed when he'd ridden that bull to victory, twice. Only this time, he'd kissed her for real. And pulled away fast. He hadn't been prepared for how much he wanted to have her. The feel of her beneath him all slick and compliant in that silk had made his brain pulsate with fire! He'd had to stop himself from…

He frowned. She hadn't seemed as rocked as he had.

So then he dove out a window. "Damn," he said again.

She was supposed to *notice*.

CISSY FORCED HERSELF not to fly to the window and peer out to see if Tex was okay. That lunatic! But what could a woman expect from a man well versed in the daredevil sport of bullriding?

"You are *so* not father material," she muttered, swiftly flipping off the bedside lamp and going to the window to surreptitiously peek through the lace drapes. He was limping, the creep! "That's what you get for being so desperate to avoid my kiss," she told his retreating form. "Now you're only worth forty bucks."

And he wasn't husband material, for sure—not

that she was looking to mine the fields of bachelors. But Tex had proved that she'd never be able to count on him. The man broke into her bedroom and then leaped out her window.

"I can't trust you," she said as he drove off. "And if I need anyone in my life right now, it's someone I can trust."

She had a family to raise. "I can just see him teaching my kids to have a wild hair like his," she murmured, picking up the picture once again. Her eyes clouded over as she looked at the faces of the tiny people who depended on her. Counted on her.

"I need stability in my life," she told herself as she crawled into bed. "Stability. And someone who doesn't call wedding cake un-wedding cake and then cut it with a hunting knife!"

Getting up, she grabbed the box off the dresser and slipped the cake under her pillow. "I'll just ignore Mr. Superstitious's dire warning," she said. "It's not like I'd dream of future husbands, anyway."

More like she'd have nightmares. Of Tex.

"WHAT'S YOUR PROBLEM?" Mason demanded as Tex limped into the ranch's main house. It was just the two of them living there now, and that fact alone was starting to string Tex's nerves tight. Mason was not a pleasant roommate.

"I just turned my ankle a bit," Tex said. "It's nothing."

Bandera and Navarro came in behind him, eyeing

Tex as he fell into the recliner and struggled to get his boot off.

"Need help?" Bandera asked.

"Not really," Tex said, gritting out the words. His ankle hurt more than he thought it would.

"Hang on," Navarro said. Gently, he took hold of the boot and did his best to pull it off without hurting Tex.

"Arrgh!" Tex moaned in spite of himself.

"Where the hell have you been?" Bandera asked. "Ranger called here a while ago and said to keep an eye out for you. Said you were three sheets to the wind last night. And then you disappeared."

"Yeah." Tex settled into the recliner, trying not to grimace at his swollen ankle. "Hannah wanted me to check on Cissy under the guise of taking her some wedding cake. So I took a shower, sobered up and hit the road."

"Ooh," his three brothers said.

"What?" Tex said, sitting up. "What does 'ooh' mean?"

"Cissy did that to you," Bandera said.

"Not exactly." But Tex didn't feel like sharing more of the story than that.

The phone rang, and Mason swept it up. "Hello?" He listened for a few moments, then said, "Yes. The superhero made it home fine. Thanks for calling." Hanging up the phone, Mason put on a fake nonchalant expression. "That was Miss Cissy Kisserton," he said, torturing Tex just a little. "She says you took a flying leap out of her bedroom window."

"Ooh," his other two brothers said.

Tex closed his eyes.

"Fear of intimacy," Navarro pronounced.

"And Ranger's Curse of the Broken Body Parts has gotten to Tex," Bandera stated. "Just look at him all laid up like that."

"What bullcorn," Mason said. "What a pile of hockey pucks."

"It's all over but the crying," Bandera said.

"Yeah, Tex crying," Navarro agreed. "We're going to have to listen to the wedding bell blues until the blood goes on the marriage certificate."

"All right. Enough," Tex said crossly. "I'm afraid you have all overstated the importance of a slightly tweaked ankle."

"Looks purple to me," Mason observed, "for a slight tweak. Think I'll ring the doc and ask him what to do for a broken ankle."

"Broken!" Tex leaned up to stare at his appendage. "It's not broken."

"You jumped out a woman's second-story window," Bandera said in disbelief, shaking his head. "The shame of it!"

Navarro blinked. "I've never heard of a Jefferson male breaking his own ankle to escape a woman."

Tex ground his teeth. "If any of you knew half as much as you think you do—"

"All we know is what we see," Navarro said. "And it's humiliating!"

"Actions speak louder than words," Bandera agreed. "Dude, your roses never move past the bud stage. You are way too out of touch with yourself and the universe to be able to release the—''

''Oh, for crying out loud.'' Tex waved a hand majestically in the air. ''You obviously have not heard the good news.''

His brothers stood by silently.

''We're going to participate in a bachelor raffle for Miss Honeycutt. Delilah. At the Mayfest.''

Navarro and Bandera stared at him, then started to howl with laughter. ''No, we're not,'' they said, leaving the room snickering.

Mason shook his head and left, as well.

''Chickens,'' Tex said, staring at his swelling ankle. Mason returned to put a bag of ice on it and then left the house.

Tex rolled his eyes. ''Fear of intimacy,'' he grumbled. ''Budus Interruptus. Curse of the Broken Body Parts. What a bunch of superstitious weirdos!''

They were *really* starting to bother him.

And Cissy bothered him even more. ''They're wrong,'' he told his ankle. ''And she's wrong. I know exactly what I'm doing. Eventually, they'll all have to admit that I'm not the one with hang-ups.''

He would unlock the Sacred Mysteries of the Rosebuds—and prove he wasn't scared of intimacy all in one fell swoop.

The raffle would be his salvation. In two weeks, he'd spend time on a date with a woman. Perfect timing for roses to bloom in glorious, take-that color.

TWO WEEKS LATER, Tex's ''tweaked'' ankle was healed, and he was on a makeshift stage at the rodeo arena. There were six men to follow him, but he didn't know them, and at this moment, he didn't care to introduce himself. He felt silly. Mimi had gussied him up; his twin, Laredo, had sent him well wishes from North Carolina; Frisco Joe had sent him roses— butthead!—and Ranger had called long distance to ask him if he could stand the stress of being owned by a woman. His still-unmarried brothers had teased him unmercifully about becoming a stud and asked him if he was going to start dancing in clubs and letting women stuff money in his G-string.

But he'd endured it all in pursuit of his goal.

Cissy Kisserton seated herself in the stands, making his every hair stand at attention, it seemed. What was it about that woman that electrified him?

She waved at him, and he jerked his head at her in a ''hello'' motion. Then she lifted a bidding paddle—prettily painted fans just for this occasion—and waved it merrily at him.

He groaned. Surely she didn't intend to carry out her threat of being a mole bidder. This was not going according to plan. He was supposed to feel liberated and free of his brothers' teasing. And he was proving to Malfunction Junction and everyone else that he wasn't an intimacy-phobe.

And there sat Cissy, looking like cool ice cream in a diamond-glazed dish.

What if she won him?

He would look sillier than he did right now. Everybody knew that Cissy was the cause of his ankle sprain, which was all it had turned out to be. His brothers would guffaw and ask what he was going to break while she collected her winnings—him.

Before the auctioneer could get rolling, Tex very pointedly shook his head at Cissy.

She nodded in return, her head bobbing with determination and a big grin on her face.

He shook his head more fiercely. And gave her the no-no-no finger.

In response, she waved her fan madly.

"Well, would you look at that anxious lady in the stands?" the auctioneer called over the microphone. "She's just determined to start the bidding! What say we open at fifty dollars for this handsome cowboy? Look him over, girls. You'll not see such chaps as these too often!"

Since he wasn't wearing chaps, Tex figured the auctioneer was referring to some portion of his anatomy. Taking a deep breath, he watched as the fans one by one moved to the quick-fire droning of the auctioneer's voice.

Up, up, up went his price.

Cissy's fan flicked with confidence.

Tex's breath hung in his chest. Surely she wasn't really trying to win him! She had no money; she'd said so herself.

The bid reached four hundred dollars, and his brothers were slack-jawed in the stands. Tex's face burned with humiliation.

"Give us a pose, cowboy!" a female called from the stands.

A pose? "Oh, come on," Tex muttered, failing to see why he should. But the audience applauded, and he decided to give them what they wanted.

He popped his arm muscles, which thanks to the short-sleeve-T-shirt Mimi had suggested, worked nicely to show off his biceps.

The ladies applauded. See? he told Cissy mentally. They notice me. Women like me, even if *you* don't.

He bent slightly at the knee and leaned forward, curling his arm so that he displayed his shoulder and forearm muscles.

The women clapped harder. "More!" someone yelled.

Emboldened, he turned around, showed the audience his backside, held his arms out to the side, and tightly flexed every muscle in his body.

The response was thunderous. With a sheepish grin, he turned back around, done with his antics.

Cissy's fan gestured wildly.

And then it seemed the arena got quiet. Buzzing hummed in Tex's ears as the auctioneer pointed to a few more fan-holding women. Tex thought maybe the lovely, dress-wearing Cissy had put her fan into her lap.

He had to admit, it wouldn't be the worst thing that ever happened to him if she won him. The woman was right sexy for a good girl. If good girls were his thing, which they weren't.

He liked his women saucy. Minx-y. A little on the bad-girl side.

Sort of the Cissy he thought he knew from their

barn encounter, before he'd found out she was newly widowed and had a mess of kids and went to church and took care of her elderly grandma.

A man couldn't poach on a gal like that, even if she did work for Marvella.

"Sold!" the auctioneer cried. "For five hundred dollars to that lady right over there!"

Chapter Four

Cissy wasn't prepared for Marvella to purchase Tex. Her heart sank. Poor Tex! His face crumbled.

She felt responsible. Enthusiastically doing her mole-bidding thing and driving up his price, she had been determined to show that she didn't care that he'd soon have a night with another woman.

It shouldn't have mattered to her, but now Marvella had her fingers in the pie. Tex wouldn't enjoy being Marvella's purchase, not at all. When she walked over to claim Tex, Cissy's skin crawled. "Wait a minute!" Cissy called out. "Marvella, can I talk to you?"

Hopping out of the stands, she went over to her boss.

"What, Cissy?" Marvella asked.

"I don't think you want to buy him," Cissy said. Tex's eyes were on her, watching her like a hawk. "He's damaged goods," she explained.

"Damaged goods?" Marvella turned to stare at the cowboy. "He's already won two rodeos for me. And he just showed us everything except his—"

"Yes, I realize that," Cissy said hurriedly. "And

it all looked fine, on the surface. But I thought you already had a cowboy for the rodeo.''

"My cowboy just came down with a bad case of running fever. He's running to Nevada, away from his ex-wife and child-support payments. This one will do better," she said with a greedy smile at Tex. "I hadn't expected him to fall into my hands."

"I'd pick the one over there," Cissy said softly. "Do you recognize him? He's the son of a retired Dallas Cowboy. And he's all the rage on the circuit. I was reading his biography in the pamphlet. He's not a has-been like this one," she said with an apologetic glance at Tex.

"I heard that!" he exclaimed. "I am not a has-been!"

She got closer to Marvella, who was looking the younger rodeo rider over with a keen eye. "Tex hurt his ankle a couple of weeks ago," Cissy said. "And his back. He just doesn't want anyone to know he's flimsy right now. Real worn down."

Marvella's head turned toward the auctioneer. "Now that I've inspected the goods up close, I rescind my bid."

And she swept away.

Tex glared at Cissy.

"Hey, I'm trying to save you," she said.

"Due to an unforeseen turn of events," the auctioneer said, "our bidder changed her mind. Does the previous bidder still want this fine cowboy gentleman? If you want to pay the former price, he's yours."

A cheer went up from the stands, and ten women

ran over to Tex, throwing themselves at him for hugs. Her rivals from the new salon in Union Junction. They were covering his face with lipstick kisses and he seemed much happier, Cissy noticed. The opportunistic louse! Well, they could have the intimacy-stunted cowboy. And his moral imperative. Plus his nicely fitting jeans and tight muscles. He wasn't that much of a prize.

"Well, I guess you're sold again, then, son," the auctioneer said. "Ten for the price of one. What a lucky guy!"

The girls squealed, thrilled. Cissy heard Tex laugh. He didn't sound so reluctant now, the ape.

Cissy walked away, telling herself she'd done the right thing.

TEX SAW CISSY LEAVING and tipped his hat to the women swarming him. "Ladies, I look forward to our night together," he said, eliciting more squeals. I'll make tonight the night of your dreams."

They ate that up.

He grinned. "I'll pick y'all up at Miss Delilah's at three o'clock, and then we'll walk to the cafeteria. I'm bringing roses for each of you."

They crowded around him, smiling. His chest expanded with pride. He could make ten girls happy at once!

But right now, he needed to take care of one. "See you then," he said, heading after Cissy. He caught her in the breezeway. "Hey. What's the hurry?"

"None, exactly." She kept walking.

He caught her hand. "So where are you going? I'd like to talk to you if you have time."

She refused to slow down. "I really don't. Sorry. I need to be minding the shop while Marvella and the other girls are gone."

"The shop's closed until tonight," he pointed out. "Everybody's at Mayfest. In fact, I was hoping to buy you some cotton candy."

"Don't like it. It's too *clingy*. Thanks."

Man, he couldn't slow her down a bit. "Cissy. Please stop."

She did, looking up at him. They stood on the sidewalk with the bright May sun washing the street in spring light, and he thought about how sweet she was. She had such a rep for being a tough cookie, but that was just her top layer. Once you got past her crunchiness, she was soft and sweet. "Thanks for rescuing me back there."

"You're welcome."

"Of course, you didn't have to make it sound like I was some over-the-hill, busted-up cowboy left-over."

"Yes, I did. Marvella's determined to beat her sister at all costs. She needed a better cowboy."

"Hey!" He tugged lightly on her long, silvery hair. "Ain't no better cowboy than this, lady."

She cocked her head. "Maybe I disagree. However, I knew you felt that this was all my fault, and so I decided to snatch you back from Marvella's jaws."

"Had me going there for a minute. Thought you

were going to buy me for yourself,'' he said with a touch of swagger.

"No." She said it calmly and with assurance. "I've already had you in my bedroom. Sparks didn't fly."

He stared at her. "They most certainly did, in the barn!"

"Maybe for you." She shrugged. "It was fun upping your price. Too bad those girls are going to be disappointed."

"What?" Now she was getting on his nerves again, just when he'd decided she was sweet and creamy!

"Well, they're expecting a fun date. And a little more."

"I'm taking them to the cafeteria. And giving them each a rose. Come on. That's not too bad for a first date, is it?"

"Did it ever occur to you that they're going to want something extra?"

"Hey, the girls will love going out for a nice meal. I mean, they seemed happy. And of course, I'll spring for dessert."

"Yes, but strawberry pie isn't the *something extra* they're going to want."

He ignored that, since he had a suspicion she might be right. In fact, he was going to have to figure out a way around kissing all those girls. "Hey, Cissy, I need to talk to you."

"We're talking, Tex."

Glancing around, he said, "In private."

"Not my room. You exit like a bad stuntman."

"You noticed?" He perked up instantly.

"Yeah. I could have heard the crash a mile away."

"Oh." He deflated again.

"And besides, I don't want anyone to get any wrong ideas about you and me."

"Meaning what?"

"That you…that we—"

"That I might be a customer?"

She stared at him. "A customer? I don't do hair, Tex. I'm not a stylist."

"That's not what I meant, exactly."

"What do you mean?"

He was getting annoyed because he didn't want to be indelicate with her. "Come on, Cissy. You know very well what the Never Lonely Cut-n-Gurls salon has a reputation for. Taking real good care of their men."

"I hope so. It *is* a service industry."

"And a little more on the service side than your average Joe's Barber Shop."

She put her hands on her hips. "Are you insinuating that I'm a good-time girl?"

That puzzled him. "Well, aren't you? Sort of? To make ends meet?"

She slapped him. "Ow! Cissy, what the hell!"

"Just slapping a little sense into you, cowboy."

"Hang on a minute." He grabbed her by her wrists and pulled her to him. "If you don't mind, I'd like a straight answer. Marvella's salon has a rep for being a whorehouse. True or false?"

She struggled against him. "I'm not friends with the other girls. I barely talk to them. They think I'm mean, and they hate me because Marvella wants me there so much. They assume I'm getting special treatment. I'm not. Marvella likes my look. She thinks I give her salon the appearance she wants it to have. I'm a hostess, you dork.''

He released her. "Dork?"

"All right. I'm sorry. But you shouldn't have implied that I was…wait a minute. Never mind. You are a dork. And a typical guy.''

"Obviously, I was wrong about everything. I apologize.''

"I don't know. I don't ask the other girls what they do with their customers. My job is to look attractive, chat sweetly and take the customers to a lady who cuts their hair, manicures them, shaves them, pedicures them, waxes them—''

"Thank you. That will do just fine.''

They stared at each other.

"I think you know it doesn't matter to me. You're still someone I want to hang around with. I do apologize,'' Tex said. "It was none of my business.''

"I bet you are sorry. Sorry that you got won by ten nice girls. If we'd thought about pooling together at Never Lonely Cut-n-Gurls, you could have been bought by a trashy bunch. And that would have been your dream come true.''

"Actually, I don't know what my dream is anymore.'' He took a deep breath. "Let me buy you lunch.''

"No, thanks.''

Damn, but she was prickly. "Here's my best and final offer, because I can tell you're really hungry.''

"I'm—"

He held up a hand to interrupt her denial. "Let me buy us some fried chicken. Then I'll drive us out to Barmaid's Creek. It's too cold to swim, but we can sit and look at the water. And I can talk to you. I promise, no hanky-panky."

She sighed. "That's not exactly an offer a girl can't refuse. So…no."

Defeated, he knew he couldn't blame her for not wanting to be with him. She'd rescued him from Marvella, and he'd repaid her by insulting her. "So. I guess we'll just talk right here. Where anybody can hear us."

"Guess so."

He nodded. "All right. I was discussing your contract with Brian, Mimi's lawyer husband because Ranger asked me to, and Brian was wondering if you had a copy of it."

She shook her head.

"Dead-end there, for the moment. Question two, about your brother and sisters, I think I know someone who would go see what can be found out about them. Someone experienced with tough conditions. Someone who knows a lot about—"

A gasp escaped her. Carefully, he watched her, wondering what her next move would be. Another slap? Ire?

He was totally unprepared when Cissy threw herself into his arms and hugged him tight. It was good, it was real good. He liked it, but he had a feeling it was about to get taken away from him. "Uh, Cissy, I meant Hawk."

She gazed up at him. "Hawk?"

"Yeah. He's experienced in tracking."

Slowly, she detached herself from him. "Oh." And then she looked delightfully embarrassed. "I'm sorry. I should have listened before I leaped."

"It's fine," he said hurriedly. "Leap anytime you like."

"Hawk," she repeated slowly. "He found me when I tried to leave town and get away from Marvella. Maybe he could find my family. Or at least find out what happened to them." She looked back up at him. "You know, that's a good idea, if you think he would."

"Why not? He's a hired tracker. Money talks."

She sighed. "Of course, I don't have the kind of money."

Tex nodded. "Well, it's something for us to look into. We could ask about the cost."

"The cost of flying to South America alone would be prohibitive. Not to mention the bribes you'd need to get information out of the locals."

"I thought about all that." He tapped her nose. "Don't give up. We can think of something."

She looked at him. "We? That's the second time you said 'we.'"

"Well, hell. You rescue me, I'll rescue you." He grinned at her. "I bet you couldn't resist sleeping with that cake under your pillow last night, could you?"

Her expression was coy. "None of your business, cowboy."

"You did. And you dreamed about someone, didn't you?"

She shook her head. "I slept like a log."

"Sleep on it again tonight. I bet you dream of me. I'm starting to get under your skin."

She laughed at him, and he was glad to hear the sound. "Remind me to spray myself with repellant the next time you fly around."

And then she walked away. Her hips switched tantalizingly, and he had to admit, that was a well-packaged woman. There were moments when he wanted to unwrap that package again.

"She's a good girl," he reminded himself.

Though there was definitely something going on between the two of them.

He just wasn't certain what it was.

"CISSY!" MARVELLA CALLED.

Cissy turned around, and she saw Tex do the same. Marvella traveled the extra fifteen feet, hauling the new cowboy with her. "Cissy, this is Ant Dilworth. Ant, meet my best girl, Cissy Kisserton."

Cissy noticed Tex had drawn within listening distance. Shame on him for being so nosy!

"Howdy, Miss Cissy," Ant said. "Kisserton's the perfect name for you. I'd kiss a gal like you a ton, if you was mine."

Marvella laughed. "Kiss her tons. I get it. Ant, you're a very smart cowboy. I like brains in a man."

Ant looked full of himself. Tex glowered. Cissy smiled.

"And this is Tex Jefferson, a local cowboy who's been kind enough to ride for our salon in the past."

The men shook hands. "Ah, yeah. You're the one she bid on first, but then decided was too tore up. Too bad, man."

Cissy tried not to giggle. But Tex's expression was priceless.

"Hey, why don't the two of you show Ant around Mayfest?" Marvella asked. "We want him to have a good time before the rodeo."

Cissy and Tex looked at each other. Ant drew himself up to his full five-foot-six height.

"All right, Marvella," Cissy said reluctantly. "Tex?"

"Well, I wouldn't dream of leaving this young man without friends," Tex said, his dark gaze on Cissy.

"Wonderful!" Marvella exclaimed. "But you have him back in good shape and on time, Cissy."

"Oh, we will." She frowned at Tex, and he raised a brow.

"Here's some spending money for my guest," Marvella said, opening her black bag. "We're good to our riders here."

"I can see that!" Ant said happily. "Getting invited to that raffle was the best thing that ever happened to me!"

"That's exactly what Tex said," Cissy fibbed, just to watch the flames explode from Tex's head. "He loves the fact that ten women won him."

"I would, too! If you decide you're too worn out

to deal with ten women, you just call me," Ant told Tex. "I'll be happy to help you out, old hoss."

"Yep," Tex said to Cissy, "I can see this is going to be as much fun as I can stand."

Marvella's sister, Delilah Honeycutt, who owned the Lonely Hearts Salon, and her friend, Jerry Martin, joined the group. "Hello, Cissy," she said to Marvella. "Tex. Thanks for coming to Lonely Hearts Station," she said to Ant. "We do appreciate your participation in the rodeo."

"Happy to be of service, ma'am," Ant replied.

Delilah turned her attention to Cissy. "I know you're aware that what started out as a charity auction for my salon turned into a lot more than we ever imagined."

"Yes," Cissy replied. "I know it's been very successful."

"More than we ever dreamed. In light of that fact, I turned in a proposal to the town council last month asking that the funds we earn go to charities in Lonely Hearts Station. The town fathers put me in charge of the Charity Selection committee, because of my position on the council and the fact that it was my idea."

Cissy wasn't surprised. The council was made up of four people: Delilah, and three elderly men who were completely loyal to her. They'd never been inside Marvella's salon, and they never would. Delilah had been in town first and had done a lot to grow the town. Marvella, to their mind, might bring in much-needed tax dollars, but she was still "new."

"Cissy, I hope you'll take this check in the spirit

that it's meant,'' Delilah said. ''I've decided that, based on what Tex has told me about your situation, you are the candidate who could benefit the most from this cowboy raffle. I'd like you to accept two thousand dollars.''

Chapter Five

Cissy sucked in a breath, and Marvella walked away, dragging Ant with her.

"I hope it will come in handy, if you decide to send someone to look for your family. I'm awfully sorry about what you're going through."

Cissy burst into tears. Tex blinked, not sure what to think about her reaction.

"Thank you so much," Cissy said. And then she hugged Delilah.

Delilah patted her back. "Well, you two go on and enjoy the rest of the day." And then she and Jerry left.

Cissy put her face on Tex's chest and sobbed like crazy. Slowly, he put his hands up to comfort her. "Hey," he said. "Don't do that. Last time you got upset, I had to compliment your butt. Who knows what I'll say this time?"

"Oh, shut up," Cissy said. "You set me up for this and you know it."

"What?"

"You know very well that I lied to your brother about which way Bloodthirsty Black cranked. I wanted

Delilah's salon to lose. I cheated. And now Delilah's giving me money. I feel so bad!''

''Well, that *was* very bad of you,'' Tex said, thinking it was funny that she'd feel so guilty. After all, Tex had figured out the problem before Laredo got his pride-bearing load kicked clean into the next county. ''Very, very bad.''

But then he stopped himself cold. ''But not that bad,'' he corrected. Not bad enough to interest him.

''Pretty bad,'' Cissy said, sniveling onto his shirt-front.

Normally, he wouldn't want a woman doing that wet-'n'-weepy thing on his shirt, but she felt kind of good tucked up against him. He was going to give her a pass, just this once, on the waterworks. ''Nah. Tiny bad.''

''Very bad!'' Cissy exclaimed, annoyed.

''Just a little wee bit. Barely noticeable bad.''

Cissy stepped away from him. ''Tex, I'm bad! Bad, bad, bad! So bad I don't think I can accept the money.''

He pulled her back to him—to comfort her as any gentleman would. ''You have to accept the money. How else are we going to get Hawk to South America?''

She looked up at him. ''You did this on purpose.''

''Well—''

''You went over there and gave Delilah a sob story so that she'd give me money.''

''Well—''

''I can't accept it, though,'' Cissy said definitively.

"That would make me really, really bad. Like, trashy bad."

He frowned. "I think you're confused on the meaning of *trashy.*"

"How?"

"Trashy's kind of a good thing. For example…" Searching for an example was always difficult where women were concerned. You had to find one that wouldn't offend, and yet one that illuminated appropriately. With Cissy, he wasn't sure which way to go.

"I've got one," she said. "That ice skater who had a competitor whacked on the knee."

"No!" She definitely didn't get that trashy was a sexy thing.

"Uh, the movie star who stole stuff."

"No, no. You're going about this all wrong. Mae West was trashy. Today's equivalent would probably be…I don't know. Girls with a little spice." He shrugged. "It's just me, you know. My brothers like the safe ones. I like the unsafe ones. They make me feel edgy."

"You are such a sicko that I'm almost attracted to you," Cissy said. "And that scares me."

"Why? I'm just looking for a good time."

She rolled her eyes. "I need to confess to Delilah before I accept this money. Your intentions were honorable, but you've flushed me out of hiding."

"So your terms are confession before donation?" He nodded. "Good, good. Very good. Definitely making up for the bad girl who lied about the left-cranking steak-on-hooves."

"Guess that makes me too good for your taste," Cissy said. "Too prim and proper."

"Not really," he said, dropping a friendly arm around her shoulders. "Since you dumped those ten stylist friends on me, you're pretty much in the cow patty as far as I'm concerned. I admire your wicked ways."

"They're not my friends," Cissy said, allowing him to walk with her to the salon, "and I didn't know who was the last bidder before Marvella. I just knew it was time for me to quit running up your price. You should have gone for about fifty, you know."

"The market bears what it will bear. We need to think up a battle plan," he told her.

"We need to take Ant around first," she reminded him.

"Did I say I was staying to help you entertain the baby-faced lad?" He glanced around. "Actually, it looks like Marvella is buying Ant some cotton candy over there." He pointed to one of the street vendors.

"Well, I don't like cotton candy. So he's lucky he's with Marvella."

"I remember you saying you don't like clingy things," he said cheerfully.

She opted to ignore the jibe. "So, what's the battle plan?"

"We need to get in touch with Hawk."

She looked up at him, trying to keep her anxiety down. The check Delilah had given her was stiff in her pocket, reminding her that this moment was real. What if Hawk couldn't find out anything about her family? What if he learned bad news? She swallowed. "And then?"

"I'll figure that out later. First, I've got a date with ten women, thanks to you. For now we need to figure out how you're going to comfort Marvella tonight when Babyface gets thrown before the buzzer. I got a real bad feeling about him, and Marvella does not like to lose."

Cissy gasped. "He can't be a bad cowboy! I read his biography in the program."

"Let me tell you two things about riding a bull, Cissy. One, even the best cowboy gets tossed occasionally. Two, the rider himself sends in that biography."

"Are you saying Ant might have padded his résumé?"

"I don't know. I've never heard of him before."

"I can't think about that right now." Cissy pursed her lips. "You could be wrong."

"I've been wrong before. But not usually about rodeoing."

She turned and headed toward Ant. "I better go take him off Marvella's hands."

"Hey, what about me?" Tex called after her.

Either she didn't hear him, or she ignored him. Tex kicked at a tiny rock in the street.

"Oh, Tex," he heard.

To his astonishment, it was Delilah calling him from the doorway of her salon.

"Yes, ma'am?" He ambled toward her.

"I've had a bit of a disaster."

Her broad face showed little sign of her usual contentment. "Is there something I can do?"

Jerry joined them in the doorway. "There is, son. You can ride Bloodthirsty Black for us tonight. Our cowboy canceled, leaving us in a bit of a pickle."

That would put Tex squarely at odds with Cissy. As much as he wanted to ride that bull for Delilah, there was a limit to what a man should do to put himself at odds with the most beautiful girl around.

Then again, things couldn't get much worse. It wasn't like they were going to have wild sex together, again, or get married and have babies.

His throat dried at the thought of Cissy. Cissy carrying a baby, preferably his. Making love to that silvery female as many times in a day as he could manage.

Boy, howdy.

Now, why would he think of Cissy like that? Maybe his brain had overheated due to all the new plans he was having to hatch.

And then again, maybe hanging around Cissy too much was enough to make a man incinerate. Thank heaven neither he nor Cissy ever wanted children. Or marriage. Or even each other.

"I'll do it," he told Delilah. "I'm not doing anything else tonight."

And if a little Ant got squashed in the process, well, that would just teach him a thing or two about the fickle nature of rodeo.

IT WAS LAST'S TURN to stay home and do the chores while everybody else drove over to Lonely Hearts

Station for the monthly fair and rodeo, but Mason gave his youngest brother the night off. There'd be a lot of fun in the little town tonight, but Mason didn't feel like looking for fun. He was worried about his next-door neighbor, Mimi, and her father, Sheriff Cannady. The brothers had recently discovered the secret Mimi had been keeping to herself. Things were more dire with the sheriff than he'd ever dreamed they could be, and the chance of finding the sheriff a new liver seemed more remote by the day. He hated to see Sheriff Cannady felled by the rogue infection that had mostly destroyed his liver—and very nearly the man.

Mimi's new husband, Brian, was a good man, but he was little help with the chores. Citified lawyers didn't usually know all that much about what needed to be done on a ranch. Mason figured he'd mosey over to Mimi's in a bit to stick his head in.

He saw the red Ferrari go by, which meant Brian was leaving for the evening. With a sigh, he realized the lawyer was probably headed to the hospital to check on the sheriff for Mimi. Which meant Mimi was home with the chores. "I'll go now," he said to himself. "Before it gets too late."

A minute later, he was on Mimi's porch knocking on the door. When she let him in, it was obvious that his childhood playmate had been crying. "Mimi! Bad news?"

He wanted desperately to take her into his arms, but he knew he couldn't. Why had Brian been leaving if Mimi was upset?

"No. No bad news." She seemed to wilt onto a

kitchen bar stool. "I just had a minute to myself, and I guess I decided to have a meltdown."

Then it wasn't about her and Brian. Good. "This is about your father."

She nodded.

There wasn't much he could say about that. The sheriff had him worried sick, too. But Mimi worried him just as much.

"I do have some good news," she said quietly. "I may be pregnant."

He blinked, and something inside him seemed to shatter. "That's…awesome, Mimi. I know you were hoping for that."

She crooked a brow at him. "How did you know that?"

"Because I know you. You're my best friend."

That put a tiny smile on her face. Mimi wanted to give her father a grandbaby; hence the hurry-up wedding with a man she'd met only recently. Mason hadn't had to think too hard to figure out what motivated his childhood friend. He reached over and wiped a tear from her cheek. "What does Brian think about becoming a father? I bet he's over the moon."

The smile faded. "Well," she said, "I think he'll be stunned."

"Stunned."

She nodded.

Oddly, Mason felt pleased that she'd told him first. Then he reigned in the inappropriate thought. "Well, I'm sure he'll be excited once the shock wears off." As far as Mason was concerned, the shock would never wear off. But he wasn't part of the marriage, so he shouldn't be feeling devastated. According to his brothers, he'd had a chance with Mimi that he'd lost forever.

Now he needed to quit being a dope. Mimi's life was moving forward. It was past time for him to pull his head out. Gently, he reached out to pat her shoulder. "Hey, I'm going to go do your chores."

She looked up at him. "You don't have to do that."

"Little mama, I'm going to be an uncle. That means you've got to take care of yourself." He grinned at her, to show her that he was the same old Mason, the brother she could count on anytime.

Then he walked out of the kitchen, knowing he had to do something to cure his stubborn heart.

"OKAY, HERE'S THE PLAN," Tex said. "I'll make good on my date with the girls, win the rodeo tonight, and then I'll apologize to Cissy," he told Last. "Then I'll hunt down Hawk and make certain he's on board for this mission."

"Hmm." Last sipped his beer as Tex examined his gear. They sat in the Lonely Hearts Station barns, so Tex could check out Bloodthirsty Black before he had to be the life of the party. "She's changing you."

"Who?" Tex glanced up.

"Cissy Kisserton."

"How so?"

"It's like you've developed Purpose in Life. Maybe that's what was missing in you. Maybe it wasn't really fear of intimacy at all. Although I do not see you making a relationship work with this woman, no matter how much she may know about the opposite sex—''

''Watch it,'' Tex growled.

''And I don't see you making a relationship work with any of the ten women who won you.'' Last crossed his legs as he sat on a beam and watched his brother. ''You know, you can be as macho as you want around the ladies and wind-and-crank them so they jump around for you like robo-girlfriends, but that's still all surface interaction. It won't get deep inside you, where the problem is.''

Tex tossed down his gloves in disgust. ''Why do you persist in thinking I have a problem? And where did you get your junior psych degree? A cereal box?''

Last shook his head with a shrug. As if to say, I tried to help you, but once again, you resisted my efforts at intervention.

''Maybe you should just take your annoying advice down the road. I've got to think about this bull. And ten women.''

''Marvella's bull was a cream puff. You haven't ridden anything like Bloodthirsty Black in a long time. Have you thought that you might not be in condition for a near-bounty bull?''

''I never underestimate the enemy, cream puff or bounty bull.''

''Hope you haven't underestimated Marvella and her Ant. And what if BadAss Blue gets out there and goes insane? Ant'll get a high score if he stays on, you know. Whilst you get thrown and tortured.''

Tex snorted.

"Have you thought of how you'll feel if you lose?"

"I don't think about losing. That's what losers do, meathead."

"Ah, I don't envy you. You're definitely stuck between a rock and a hard place," Last said, leaning back and cracking open another beer. "If you win, you'll get Cissy in big trouble. After all, she told her boss you were a has-been in order to save you. And if you lose, well, you won't look very manly to Cissy. No man does when he's being flung and stomped like a straw doll. And losing would be tough luck for Delilah. I've never forgotten how those ladies of hers helped us out during the Big Storm." He sighed dramatically. "Well, we Jeffersons do remember our friends in times of need. At least you did the charity raffle for Delilah. That's *something*. Even if the girls end up wondering what exactly it was that they won."

Tex hesitated, not happy with what he was hearing. "Maybe you should shut up now."

Last shrugged again, his face wreathed with mirthful devilment.

Tex glared.

"I checked your roses yesterday," Last said. "Such tight little buds. So afraid of coming out of their little satiny cocoons."

"Damn it!" Tex leaped on his brother, tossing him to the ground. They went rolling and kicking and punching and cursing through the straw and heaven knew what else as they tried to kill each other.

"Hell's bell's!" Navarro said as he walked in with Archer.

"Should we let them blow off some steam?" Archer asked. "Or do we get a bucket of cold water and separate them?"

On the floor, Tex and Last were locked in a titanic wrestling match for brotherly superiority.

"Lotta anger in there," Navarro observed calmly. "I'll set my watch for another two minutes."

"However, Last is the baby," Archer pointed out. "Mason would not like Tex beating up on the baby."

"All right. Set for a minute, then."

Cissy walked in and stood in the middle of the aisle, frozen by the sound of grunts and the image of immaturity on the floor. "What is happening?" she asked Navarro and Archer.

"Warm-up for bull-riding," Navarro said with a grin. He tipped his hat. "I'm Navarro Jefferson."

"I'm Archer Jefferson."

"I'm Cissy Kisserton," she said, and they both eagerly shook her hand. "Does Tex always warm up like that?"

"Oh, yes," Archer assured her. "Gotta loosen up the joints, stretch the muscles. You know. It's why Tex is so good at what he does. He insists upon this routine before every ride."

Tex let out a particularly loud yell and a potent curse. Cissy gasped.

Navarro said, "Time," and Archer called, "Oh, Tex, Cissy's here with a basket of chocolate chip cookies for you," and Tex leaped to his feet as if he'd been shot out of a cannon.

Last rolled over and eyed Cissy, slowly getting to his feet. "Howdy, ma'am," he said politely, his tone that which one uses for royalty. "I'm Last Jefferson. I do not believe we've met, but may I say that what I've heard about you pales when compared to meeting you face-to-face."

"That's so sweet," Cissy said, charmed. "How kind of you."

The three other Jefferson brothers groaned.

"Tex," she said, "here's some cookies I baked for you."

He puffed up instantly. Let Last see that he was capable of intimate acquaintance with a woman! "My favorite. Thank you, sugar."

And then he kissed her on the lips. Lightly. As if he did it all the time.

She glared at him.

He blinked at her fast, trying to signal an SOS.

"Tex Jefferson, if these were fortune cookies, they'd say 'If you ever do that again, you won't have a bright future,'" she whispered. "Or any future. Or parts of your body left to ride with. Get the picture?"

"Hey, you save me, I save you."

"When did we make that deal?" she demanded. "Isn't there an expiration on implicit deal-making?"

"I don't know! Work with me, okay?"

He took her silence as stiff acquiescence. "Now, you run along," he told her. "A barn's no place for a pretty girl like you."

His three brothers groaned, and Cissy squashed his

toe with her shoe as she walked by. He saw stars but still managed to watch her walk out of the barn. Swish, sway, moving like magic. Fact was, he'd rather she stayed, but with these brothers of his around, he wouldn't be able to relax, and then he'd make a huge mess of everything. He could feel them weighing his every move, assessing his manliness and aptitude with the ladies. It was all he could do to act normal, when he felt so many puzzling things about Cissy.

"Hey, smooth operator," Navarro said, "share some of those cookies with us."

Tex snatched the basket away. "No dice. Y'all are getting on my nerves. Especially you," he said to Last. Last stared at him silently. His youngest brother had straw sticking out of his hair, and Tex figured he didn't look much better. It was just his luck that Cissy would walk in when he was rolling around on the ground. "In fact, if y'all can't be helpful, why don't you get the hell out of here. I'm not liking you very much at the moment."

Silently, they filed out. Tex set down the basket he'd been protecting and looked at Cissy's handiwork.

It was the most thoughtful thing a woman had ever done for him, right up until she'd squashed his toe and threatened his manhood.

Which he richly deserved.

He didn't act like himself around Cissy, and it was worse with his brothers around. There was no relaxation. His brain was on full buzz the instant he saw her, heard her, smelled her.

And yet, he couldn't seem to do anything to rev down his senses.

Maybe Last was right, the little turd.

It was too horrible to contemplate.

And then he realized something. Cissy had known he was riding for Delilah tonight or she wouldn't have brought the cookies. She hadn't seemed surprised at all when his brothers talked about warming up. Stretching. What had Last said about Cissy being in big trouble if Tex won for Delilah's salon?

He stared at the cookies, suddenly suspicious.

"Nah," he said. "She wouldn't dream of it!"

There were times to be prudent. There were times to kick back and enjoy the good things in life.

The scent of the cookies wafted to him, warm and inviting and the sweetest thing a woman had ever done for him.

Last's face popped into his mind, chiding him, deriding him about the tight little rosebuds. Last would probably say this moment of paranoia was brought on by Fear of Intimacy.

Tex popped a cookie into his mouth, chewing happily, tasting love and happiness and the good feeling the work of a woman's hands can bring. No fear of intimacy here; he'd consume every bit of her offering.

And he kept consuming until the basket was empty. "Now all the love's in my tummy!" he told his pride. "And I feel…ill."

Chapter Six

After Cissy left the barn, she headed over to the Lonely Hearts Salon to speak to her benefactress, Delilah. Cissy's conscience would not allow her to take the money without confessing what she'd done back in March.

It wasn't going to be easy.

When she walked into the salon, the hush that fell was ominous. Sprayers quit spraying, gossip stopped, foils ceased being pulled for highlights. She was, after all, from the enemy camp and, therefore, the enemy. Delilah's salon had been the first in town, and was legitimate. And her girls were honest.

Cissy refused to lower her gaze. "Could I speak to Delilah?" she asked the room at large.

"I'll get her," someone said.

Cissy waited uncomfortably until Delilah called to her from a hallway. "Come this way, Cissy. Join me and Jerry in the kitchen. I'm trying to whip up a fruit salad."

Cissy gave a slight wave to the women in the salon and crossed into the part of the building that was used as a house for the stylists. Well separated from the salon, it was quiet and cozy. Just like she'd always imagined it would be.

She would have liked working for Delilah.

"Hello, Cissy," Jerry said.

"Can I offer you some tea?" Delilah asked.

Cissy shook her head, nervous. "No, thank you."

"Take a seat," Jerry told her.

"I better stand, I think." Cissy looked into both of their kind faces and felt terrible. "I have something I want to tell you before I accept the donation."

They looked at her, waiting patiently.

Cissy took a deep breath. "When Laredo rode your bull, I gave him a bad tip."

They were silent.

"I told him Bloodthirsty Black went left out of the chute so he'd be unprepared and fall off." She didn't mention that the Jeffersons had figured her out before Laredo ever got into the chute. Her intentions were what mattered.

"Well," Delilah said, "I'm glad you told me."

"I had to."

Delilah nodded. "I hope you're able to send someone who can find out something about your family, Cissy."

Cissy stared at her. "I feel that I should return your donation."

"No. You're far more honest than many people in this town. And you have a real need. You deserve it."

Jerry nodded in agreement.

"Thank you," Cissy said softly.

"Anyway, the Cissy you are now wouldn't do

such a thing. The Cissy I see before me is a changed girl, one I'd be proud to have working for me when you finish your contract with Marvella.''

"I'm not changed. Not really," Cissy said miserably. "There are some days when I feel so mean.''

"Trapped animals are mean. In that kind of situation, so are humans. Anyway, your sweet side is winning. And I think it has a lot to do with that cowboy.''

She could only be talking about one man. "Tex?"

Delilah shrugged with a smile.

Cissy shook her head. "Actually, I think I'd be making big headway into the sweeter side of my personality if he weren't around. He seems to bring out conflicting emotions in me. I see him, and I want to smile. But then he opens his mouth, and I want to slap him. Or he does something, and I want to kill him. Truly, I don't think he's the good influence you think he is.''

Jerry and Delilah laughed.

"Isn't love grand?" Delilah said to Jerry. They shared a conspiratorial wink.

"Love?" Cissy backed away from the table. "Um, I have to take one of Marvella's guests around town for a quick tour. Thank you for letting me talk to you, Delilah. I guess we'll see each other tonight.''

She left in a hurry. Love? No, love was not what she felt for that quixotic cowboy. Okay, so maybe at one time she might have confused herself on that point, but ever since he'd shown his true colors by saying he couldn't handle her squadron of children, she'd known she would never love a man like him.

Conspirators, that's what they were. She was in conspiracy, but she wasn't in *love*.

The way she felt about Tex, it was every conspirator for themselves.

"SHE POISONED ME!" Tex told Navarro, Last and Archer as they hovered around him in one of Delilah's upstairs bedrooms. He lay in a bed, feeling real green around the gills.

He heard a sigh of impatience from his brothers.

"Oh, yeah, Cissy Kisserton is the kind of woman who would put a lot of thought into poisoning a man," Archer said. "I sensed she was that kind of girl last month when we were on the road trip with Hannah and Ranger. Hell, Tex, practically the only thing she did on the whole ride was read those, you know, ladies' mags with the recipes and columns to the lovelorn. She's into cooking and womanly stuff, not poisoning freaky garden gnomes."

Tex closed his eyes. "Laxatives. The chocolate kiss of death. She probably has her own special recipe."

"Yeah, she's got those black widow sensibilities," Navarro said. "I bet she even calls that recipe her Love Potion for Sad Sacks."

"No, Tex," Last said impatiently. "You're just once again thinking of a way out of intimacy with a woman. Every female knows that the way to a man's heart is through his stomach. Of course, that's what their mothers tell them so they won't realize the real way to our hearts. But I digress. So she baked for you. And you pay back her kindness by developing a phantom gut ache. You know, Tex, you are so uncomfortable around women that it's annoying!''

"Women!" Tex tried to sit up and then fell back with a groan, the cramping in his stomach too intense. "I've got a date with ten women in a few minutes!"

"Well, there you have it," Navarro said with disgust. "Once again, you are right, little Jefferson therapist. I wish I'd put money on the fact that he'd figure a way out of going out with ten beautiful women. I'da made a fortune."

"I didn't do this on purpose!" Tex said, clutching his stomach. "She poisoned me so I wouldn't win tonight."

"How you gonna ride a bounty bull when you can't stop moaning and groaning?" Archer demanded. "None of us are prepared to do this for you, I can tell you. We're here to have a good time."

"Well," Last said philosophically as he glanced into the mirror. He checked his hair, tucking it behind his ears, and then borrowed some mouthwash from the medicine chest in the bathroom. "I, for one, do not intend to let down ten women, who are friends of ours, who helped us out during one of the worst floods ever to befall Union Junction. No, I don't."

"Me, neither," Navarro said, copying his brother's penchant for the mouthwash. "I'm positive they won't be too disappointed to get three strong, whole Jeffersons instead of one puny one."

Archer looked at him with shame. "You're on your own, sickly one. We'll see you later, bro."

"Don't worry," Last said as they walked out the

door. "Once again, we don't mind taking up your responsibilities."

"Why?" Tex asked on a groan. "Why was I born into this family? Never again do I want a big family!"

When this was all over, he was going to become a hermit. Once he'd delivered Cissy from Marvella, as Hannah had pleaded with him to do—and did what he could to find out what happened to Cissy's family—he was going to buy his own hundred acres and live there. Alone.

He'd had enough of family ties.

ON THE WAY TO THE CAFETERIA, the brothers ran into Cissy Kisserton. "Hey, Cissy," they said.

"Hi," she replied.

They smiled at her with sneaky enthusiasm. "Guess where Tex is?"

She looked at them. "Why should I care?"

"Because he's rolling around in bed claiming you poisoned his cookies with laxatives," Last said cheerfully. "He thinks you want him to lose tonight."

Navarro grinned. "Or that you didn't want him to go out with those ten rivals of yours. So we're going to do it for him."

"Yeah, it's a total sacrifice on our parts," Archer said. "He's such a pig that he ate every one of those cookies, and then he wonders why he's got a boilermaker between his ribs. His loss, our gain."

"What a dope," Last said. "We sure hope you don't feel compelled to feel guilty about this, Cissy."

She backed up a step. "Well, not really. Where is he?"

"Upstairs in a room at Delilah's. Feeling sorry for himself, mostly. If you go up the backstairs, you'll find him in the third room on the right. You'll know it by the sound of pain," Last said cheerfully. "See ya tonight, and good luck to your salon's bull."

"We woulda said Tex would win tonight, but now we figure the handicap is in play," Archer said. "All bets are off due to irregular circumstances."

"I see." Cissy flew up the stairs.

Last glanced at his two brothers. "Hey, did it seem like she was in a hurry?"

Archer stared after the beautiful woman. "Yeah, it did."

"Almost as if she…cared about our pinheaded brother?" Last wondered.

"It did seem as if she was in a rush to get up there." Navarro stared at his brothers, sharing their surprise.

"Then again, didn't Tex mention that she took care of her nieces and nephews? Maybe he arouses her mothering spirit."

"What else would she see in him?" Archer asked. "Tex doesn't have the first clue about romancing a woman."

CISSY HURRIED UP THE backstairs and went to the door the Jefferson men had mentioned. She knocked on it. "Tex?"

"What?"

"It's Cissy. Can I come in?"

"No."

Either he really thought she'd poisoned him, or he was in pain. She doubted he had company, but it was probably best to clear that hurdle. "Are you alone?"

"Yes, and staying that way for the rest of my life!"

"Whatever," she said under her breath. "Here goes nothing." Opening the door, she poked her head in. The room was dim, and in the bed she could see a lump. Quietly, she shut the door. "Tex? Are you all right?"

"Funny you should ask. How did you get in here?" he demanded, rolling over to look at her.

"Same way you got into my room when you weren't welcome. Can I get you something?"

"I think you've done enough."

"I did not poison you."

He turned to look at her again. "What makes you think I think that?"

"Your brothers told me."

"Of course. Judases to the core."

She sat on the bed next to him. "Can I get you some Tums or something? I'm sure Delilah's got something I could ask her for."

"I'm fine now. In fact, I'm starting to feel much better. 'Course, there for a while, it was touch and go."

She smiled. "I'm sorry."

"No, you're not. You're happy to see me miserable."

"Well, maybe just a little. It takes your attitude down a notch."

He looked at her. "I ate every one of those damn cookies. Every single one."

"And then you wonder why you got a stomach-ache, Einstein."

"Actually, I've decided it was something else I ate that had been sitting in my truck too long."

"With all the food at Mayfest, you snacked on something out of your truck?" She felt his forehead, which actually felt pretty good to her. Maybe because it was him.

"I was a little hungry. This was before you'd brought the cookies. Actually, it was before the raffle, even. It seems like hours ago."

"Go to sleep," she said. "You'll need all your strength for the rodeo. I'll get you some ginger ale. Later, you can apologize for spreading stupid rumors about my cooking. And use your good manners to thank me for wishing you good luck with the cookies. You know, I could have baked for Ant, since, technically, he's my rider."

"Do you believe that the way to a man's heart is through his stomach? My brothers say that's what women think."

"Well, my Gran always said that's the way it works."

"In that case, you were trying to kill me," he said with a sigh. "You were trying to tell my stomach exactly how you felt about me, and my heart has heard the news."

She rolled her eyes. "You did this to yourself. I'm going to get that ginger ale now."

He closed his eyes and put a hand on her wrist. "No. Stay with me."

She hesitated. "Um—"

"You've heard what babies men are when they're sick."

He didn't look like a baby. He looked like a six-foot-four-inch hunk stretched out on the bed, staring at her with dark hair falling into those gorgeous eyes. This was a man who could make a baby any time he put his mind to it. Her pulse sped up uncomfortably.

"Or we could buck the trend," he suggested, and she had the suspicion that he was ogling her a bit. "Let me baby you, baby."

Her pulse kicked into crazy time. "I think that might stretch the boundaries of our conspiratorial relationship—"

"Cissy, shut up," he said, pulling her into the bed and tucking her against him. "You have no sense of humor whatsoever. Now, let me get some rest."

Her eyes went huge. He was warm all along the back of her, and there were places on him touching places on her, intimately.

"Hmm," he said. "You make my stomach feel better. Like a hot water bottle. By the way, do you want me to lose?"

"No," she said, and he said, "Good girl," and then dropped a featherlight kiss on the back of her neck. She closed her eyes tightly. No. He had not kissed her. His chin had touched her, or his cheek, or his nose, but it was nothing more than that. Or he was really ill. That was it—a comfort kiss.

But it was clear his brothers were wrong about

Tex's fear of intimacy. He wasn't afraid of being close to her.

Tex might not be afraid, but *she* was afraid of being close to him. Stiffly, she lay in his arms. She thought about her marriage, which hadn't been much of a marriage. And then she thought about her family. Nine little faces and Gran. Her three siblings, whom she was terrified she might never see again.

Tex breathed softly into her hair and muttered something that sounded like "poison."

She unstiffened and made herself relax by thinking about the riverboat she'd been on last month with Hannah and Ranger and the riverboat captain, Jellyfish. Even though she'd been there only a short time before Marvella found her, she'd been happy. Something about that riverboat had made her feel relaxed and at peace, the same way she felt at Gran's. Maybe it was the water. Maybe it was the sensation of gentle movement. But there was peace and beauty all around, surrounding her with calm. She could see why Hannah had married Ranger there. She wished she could have been at the wedding.

If she had a dream come true, it would be to own a riverboat like that and float forever. There were so many things in her life right now that were upside down. She couldn't seem to stop worrying. But the cowboy muttering sleepy words in her hair had decided to take up her cause. And just being around him made her feel as if she was going to make it— somehow.

Of course, he made her crazy, too. They were not

the people they needed to be to make each other happy.

She didn't want him to lose.

But she didn't want him to win, either.

Chapter Seven

When Tex awakened, Cissy was gone. His brothers were eyeballing him, which wasn't what he'd hoped to see upon opening his eyes. He'd planned on lapping up the lovely Cissy, but that fantasy was dashed thanks to the constant familial fog surrounding him.

"How do you feel?" Last demanded.

"Better when I had a girl in here." He sat up, annoyed. "Did you scare her off?"

"No. Guess you didn't have sufficient lockdown on her. Hey, it's show time, bro," Navarro said. "By the way, we enjoyed your date. Dates."

Archer looked at his irritated brother. "We've rethought our position on helping you out. We don't want you getting killed by that bull. One of us'll ride for you. Consider it family duty. Brother salvaging brother."

"Nope." He felt much better since he'd napped with Cissy. All that body warmth against him had soothed his innards. Of course, she'd put a knot in him somewhere else, but that was a good thing. Made him feel like he was alive. Made him feel like riding a bull. Ten bulls, for that matter. "I can do my own job. Thanks, though." He went to wash up.

When he came out, his brothers were perched on his bed. "What?"

Last handed him a couple of sheets of paper. "Cissy wanted us to give you this. We ran into her at the Never Lonely Cut-n-Gurls."

"I thought you were out on my dates, not shopping the competition. Is this a contract?" Tex glanced over the papers with surprise.

"We *were* on your dates. But the girls were talking so much about how they despised the Cut-n-Gurls that we decided we had to see what all the uproar was about. So after our luncheon—including the roses you promised, and a little bit of table-dancing—we poked our heads in there. That's quite a setup," Last said with admiration. "I wouldn't mind a trim."

His brothers guffawed. Tex glanced up from the document. "This is Cissy's contract with Marvella."

"Apparently so." Navarro shrugged. "Cissy said she filched it while Marvella was busy with Ant. She said you wanted it."

"I do. I want Brian to look it over. Can you go make a copy?" Tex asked. "I think it's best if I don't ride off with the only document in existence."

"Might not be the only one," Archer pointed out. He pulled out a lighter and shot a stream of fire from it. "You know, when things disappear, no one can prove that they ever existed."

They all chewed on that for a moment. But matters couldn't be solved by his brother the flame fairy.

"Marvella's too shrewd," Tex said. "I doubt she has only one original and no copies. It's too risky."

"What's Brian going to do with it?" Navarro asked.

"I'm hoping he'll find a loophole to get Cissy out of the contract. There's no reason she should have to stay there if she doesn't want to."

"She can quit," Last said.

"Not without financial repercussions. And besides, you don't know Marvella. She's witchy." Tex handed the document to Navarro. "I trust you to guard this with your life. Get a copy, and then sneak the original back to Cissy. During the rodeo, when Marvella will be gone. This is a top-secret mission. Do not screw it up."

The brothers grinned.

THE BEAUTIFUL WEATHER brought out a record number for the Mayfest. Tex would have enjoyed the moment, except that he was undecided. Racked. Torn.

Cissy had been the only one who cared to comfort his cramping gut, and then she'd fallen asleep with him so peacefully—or maybe it was he who'd fallen asleep so sweetly. But when he'd held her he'd thought over his brothers' debate.

Win or lose?

It was an onerous question. Marvella would probably be angry with Cissy if he won. But it wasn't fair to Delilah not to give it his best shot. He figured that since he wasn't feeling a hundred percent, and he was riding a bull that was legendary—no one had stayed on Bloodthirsty yet—the odds were about even.

Yet it seemed about time that the Lonely Hearts gals racked up a win. He was not a has-been. Nor was he intimacy-stunted.

He had something to prove. Girded for battle emotionally, he left his room and grabbed his gear out of the bin in his truck. Then he crossed the street, heading for the arena.

Ant accosted him on the way. "Hey, ol' hoss!"

"Hey," Tex said, wondering when he'd become an ol' hoss in the stable of life.

"You ready for this?" Ant asked.

"I am," Tex replied with determination.

"That Marvella sure is a nice lady," Ant said. "I'm ready to win this for her."

Tex gave the younger cowboy a jaundiced eye. "You give it your best shot. But just remember, age before beauty."

Ant glared at him. "Are you insultin' me?"

"Just stating the facts, young hoss." And then he went inside to change.

AFTER PLEADING A HEADACHE, which she actually had, Cissy sat at the reception desk of the Never Lonely Cut-n-Gurls salon, waiting anxiously for the call from Valentine, who'd promised to update her. If Tex won, Cissy was going to be in big trouble. On the other hand, if he lost, Marvella was going to be very pleased with her.

As much as she liked Tex, Cissy really needed Marvella happy. Now that she'd actually stolen the contract, Cissy didn't want there to be any reason Marvella might go looking for it. Her stomach turned inside out. Even though it was *her* contract, it wasn't her property, and she felt ill from pilfering it.

It had been an act of desperation. She'd known she had to do it, once Tex held her in his arms. There would never be anything between them as a couple. But she no longer wanted to be tied to a woman she despised and a job she didn't feel right about. When Tex had asked her about the salon being a whorehouse, she'd had to face what she had always chosen to ignore.

She'd known there was something more going on than was right. Nine little children and Gran deserved better from her than this. Yes, she'd felt the weight of responsibility once her siblings went missing. Yes, she'd been scared when her husband had disappeared and the accounts had mysteriously closed. She wasn't in his will, of course, as their marriage was a document, not a promise of forever.

If Tex could find a way for her to break Marvella's contract, she was getting out. And this was the last time she'd ever hope for a rescue from a man.

It was time for her to start over.

"Hey, Cissy," Last said as he poked his head around the door. "Coast clear?"

"Yes." But she still tossed an anxious glance over her shoulder.

He and Navarro strolled in and surreptitiously handed her the contract. "We made a copy. Tex thought it was best if you put this back."

Relief flooded her. "Why didn't I think of that? I could have gone to the post office and made a copy."

"Never mind," Navarro said with a shrug. "Tex has good ideas occasionally."

"Go tuck that away where it belongs and then walk over to the rodeo with us. If we hurry, we should catch our cowboys' rides." Last grinned at her. "Tex looked ready to rock after his nap."

"That should make me feel better, but unfortunately, it doesn't. It's a good news/bad news thing." She hopped up from the desk and hurried down the hall, slipping into Marvella's office. Sticking the contract back where it belonged, she shut the file drawer and left. "That's the last thing I steal. Stealing is not good for my heart rate."

The brothers were examining the heart-shaped hot tub when she returned to the lobby. "That's a doozy," Last said. "Must have some real fun in that pool. I've seen cricks smaller than that."

Cissy grimaced. "Marvella likes her customers to be comfortable."

"Marvella likes her customers to have room to swim," Navarro said. "You could have a whale show in there."

"Where's Archer?" Cissy asked.

"Helping Tex. We couldn't leave him to his own devices." Last couldn't take his attention from the hot tub. "What's this?" he asked, picking up a plastic bottle from a shelf. "Madame Mystery's Mystical Mood Magic." He stared at Cissy. "What the hell does that mean?"

"I don't know," Navarro said, joining his brother

to examine the bottle. "But I think I gotta get me some."

"Come on," Cissy said, flushing. "We're going to miss your brother's ride."

Last set the bottle down reluctantly. "Okay. Although eventually, I'm coming back here for my own swim."

"Fine, fine." Cissy hurried to the front door. She glanced behind her at the brothers who were definitely sidetracked by the salon's accoutrements. They had no perception of the balance that her life was hanging in right now—and that their brother was going to tip the scale one way or the other. "Funny how I've developed a real love of rodeo in the past few months. Come on!"

FROM THE MOMENT TEX laid eyes on Bloodthirsty Black, he could tell the bull was ready to tear him into bite-size chunks. The cowboys had a helluva time getting the bull into the chute, and one man was in the corner nursing a hand that had gotten caught by a horn. Once Bloodthirsty was in, Archer helped Tex on, cussing and grunting as he hung from the rails of the chute.

"Hang on tight!" Archer shouted at Tex. "Stay with him."

Tex nodded and clamped his hat down hard with his free hand. His other was wound into the lifeline between him and the bull. Only one of them was going to live through this battle with honor. He'd seen Cissy come in with his brothers and sit on Delilah's side of the arena. Marvella was seated with her girls on the opposite side. It felt like the nearest to the old Roman coliseum as he'd ever get. And he was the gladiator.

"Come on, you pasty-faced, weak-spined creature," he said, his teeth rattling, his muscles bouncing as Bloodthirsty tried to shrug him off with a massive lift even though he was still inside the chute. Tex would have sworn his liver exploded and a chip got knocked off his front tooth.

The cowboys around him shouted, and someone yelled something at him, but he could no longer hear. Adrenaline had shut down all his senses except the tactical need to stay attached to the thing under him. The gate swung open, and Bloodthirsty charged out.

The bull was aiming to send him to hell.

CISSY GASPED WHEN Bloodthirsty Black leaped from the chute with a hapless Tex clinging to him. She grabbed Last's hand, feeling every turn, every jolt, every blow herself. The bull twisted and wheeled, jumped and kicked, and still Tex hung on. Left, right, up, down—Cissy could only watch with sick dread.

It was the longest eight seconds in her life.

And then Tex was flung off, a second past the buzzer. He ran up the corral, holding on until two clowns chased Bloodthirsty out of the arena. Then he got down to thunderous applause from Delilah's team, no one applauding more wildly than Cissy.

Until she saw Marvella and her girls staring across the arena at her. The furious look on Marvella's face, even at this distance, clearly said, "Traitor."

"Ninety-one!" the announcer called. "What a ride

from Tex Jefferson! Who'da thought that cowboy still had it in him for a legendary bull like Blood-thirsty Black? Give him a hand, friends! He's the first cowboy to stay on that son of a gun and deserves every point of that score!''

Cissy put her hands down. Ant still had to ride, and if she was smart, she'd best go across and sit where she belonged. Especially since she'd convinced Marvella that Tex was sub-par.

In rescuing Tex from Marvella, she might have delivered herself into big trouble.

Ant just had to win. She hoped he hadn't overstated his biography. ''I'll see you guys later,'' she told Tex's brothers.

''Hey, hang on. Where are you going?'' Last asked. ''I'm sure Tex will be over here in a sec.''

She shook her head. ''I need to go sit with my employer. Bye, everybody. Tell Tex I said…congratulations.''

She left, and Last and Navarro looked at each other. ''Congratulations? What the hell did that mean?'' Navarro asked Last.

Last shrugged and ate some popcorn. ''I think it means, congratulations, my cookies didn't kill you, you toad.''

''WHERE'S CISSY?'' TEX ASKED, leaping into the seat Cissy had vacated and receiving pats on the back and congratulations from the Lonely Hearts girls sitting all around. They hugged and kissed him, and Delilah beamed. Jerry grinned from ear to ear. It was worth feeling as if his tailbone had come unhinged to bask in the glory of these people's gratitude. They deserved that win, and after what they'd done for Union Junction, he was proud to be the one to give it to them.

It felt damn good. "Where's Cissy?" he repeated as Jerry happily slapped him on the back.

"Oh, she went to sit with her crew," Last said nonchalantly. "But she did say to tell you congratulations."

Tex frowned. "Congratulations?" What the hell? He wanted a kiss from that girl! He wanted a hug at the very least, so that he could squash her warm body up against his and enjoy every centimeter of her flesh pressed tightly to him.

Of course she wasn't *his* girl, but—

"Huh?" he said, realizing Last was droning in his ear.

"I said it looks like the Frigidaire is freezing your friend."

Tex looked over to Marvella's side of the arena. She turned her head when Cissy sat down and then didn't acknowledge her at all. In fact, Marvella adjusted her posture so that she created distance between them.

"Why does she have to be such an old bat?" Tex asked. The three brothers were sitting together so that no one else could hear them, and Tex felt free to express himself.

"Oh, you remember—the sister problem," Last said.

Tex's attention went to the next cowboy bursting

from the chute. "Uh, whatever. What was the sister problem again?"

Last clucked as the cowboy hit the dirt before the buzzer. "Anyway, supposedly Delilah stole Marvella's husband. And Marvella's been on her case ever since. Has to beat Delilah at everything."

Tex blinked and glanced back at Cissy, who was still a pariah among her own. "I'd forgotten about the bad blood. I knew Marvella would want to win, and that she'd be angry because Cissy had talked her out of buying me at the raffle, but this is just a game, you know. It's just for fun."

"And money, and buckles, and kisses and hopefully sex," Navarro said. "However, I think it's safe to say that you ain't getting any. Kisses or sex, that is. You might win the money and the buckle, depending on what Ant does."

Across the arena, Cissy's sad eyes locked onto his.

"I couldn't lose," Tex said. "For all the obvious sentimental reasons, and then the fact that it's a man thing."

His brothers stared at him, digesting. "True," they said.

"But then again, it might have been cricket to let your gal pal look good to her boss," Last offered. "Then you might have gotten sex. This way, you're going to get the cold shoulder. But I would expect *you* to be more focused on the ego thing than the sex thing."

"Spare me," Tex said, watching another cowboy get flung to the dirt and then get chased up the rail by a bull. "A man's gotta do his job. There's no guarantee of a woman's affections."

"Not the way you go at it," Navarro agreed.

Tex shrugged. He'd done what he had to, and he wouldn't have done it any other way. Even if he'd still had the stomachache, he would have gotten up there and ridden the hell out of any bull presented to him. It was the right thing to do.

Ant jumped out of the gate on BadAss Blue, and it seemed all the Lonely Hearts ladies leaned forward as one. Blue jumped and thrashed, buckled and blew, but it was no knuckle-popper of a show like Bloodthirsty had put on. Finally the buzzer sounded. Ant jumped off, heading away from the bull and onto a gate until Blue had been safely steered out.

The whole building went silent, waiting.

"Seventy-nine!" the announced called. "Tex Jefferson easily wins the championship! Same cowboy, different bull, different salon, and he still gets the job done. Hurray for the man from Malfunction Junction!"

People slapped Tex on the back and cheered and called his name. Across the arena, he saw Cissy leave, and then Marvella and her crew filed out. It wasn't hard to miss the animosity radiating across the sawdust and bleachers.

His brothers looked at him stoically.

"Let me repeat Cissy's congratulations," Last said. "And let me spell this out for you—you won the man thing, and lost the girl. You dummy."

Chapter Eight

Cissy could feel the heat of Marvella's stare on her as they left the arena. In silence, the group of women returned to the salon. Cissy headed upstairs to her room without speaking to anyone.

She didn't feel guilty about what she'd done at all. None of it. Rocks pelted her window, and she looked out. "Tex! Haven't you gotten me into enough trouble?"

"No! Come out and congratulate me!"

"You're crazy! If Marvella sees me leave with you, she's going to think there's a conspiracy. Or that I'm happy you won."

He cocked his head at her, looking devilishly sexy and delighted with himself. "Aren't you?"

There was no need to reply to that. "Stop fishing for applause. Don't you have something better to do than stand in the street and yell at me?"

"No." He grinned up at her. "Is she going to send you to bed without supper? If she is, I'll be happy to take you out. It's the least I can do to thank you for, you know...the great rescue."

"You don't need to thank me."

"So I don't want to eat alone. Come with me."

"Last I checked, there were ten women eager to share a meal with you. I'm sure they're across the street visiting with their sisters and enjoying their first win."

"Yeah, but I'd rather eat with one cool chick than ten okay chicks."

Cissy stared at him. Why now? Why him? Finally, she said, "Go away, Tex. You're making my life more difficult than it needs to be." And she shut the window.

TEX STARED DOWN AT HIS boots as Cissy disappeared from view. She was right. He was making her life more difficult. Why, though? All he wanted to do was help her, rescue her, to fulfill his obligation to his new sister-in-law, Hannah.

But Last was right: she didn't want anything to do with him. And Tex couldn't blame her. He'd won the battle and lost the war.

He so badly wanted to change that. "Well, hell. You win, you lose, and sometimes you do them both at the same time. Rare talent, that."

There was nothing more for him here. He glanced up at Cissy's window one more time, but it was shut tighter than a virgin's legs and wasn't going to open for him anytime soon.

Sighing, he headed to his truck. He made certain his gear was secured, then looked around for his brothers' truck. They had vamoosed. It was time for him to do so as well. By now, back home, his roses should be blooming. At least there was *something* for him to look forward to at Malfunction Junction.

Inside the truck, on the car seat, was the copy of Cissy's contract.

He'd drop that off with Brian before he checked on the roses, he decided. Just in case there were so many blooms that he got excited and forgot that he was supposed to be an award-winning cowboy. He'd won a trophy, a buckle, lots of kisses from Delilah's girls—on the cheek, of course—and Delilah's gratitude.

Hannah had asked him to help Cissy out of her contract. Delilah had asked him to ride her bull. "One down, one to go," he said. "And then I'm going to take photographs of my extremely hot roses. That's all I want, to look at my colorful beauties while my body recovers."

And maybe Brian could figure out something to do about Cissy. Because Tex was certainly coming up with zeroes.

AT MALFUNCTION JUNCTION, there wasn't a lot of excitement over Tex's win. Mason barely looked up from his newspaper when Tex walked in. The other brothers, who'd by now been prepped by Navarro and Last and Archer, gave a few claps but then focused on their Pokeno game. .

Pokeno. Who wanted to play a game like that? Of course, it was one of the few games that they all could play together. Their father, Maverick, had used the game to make them focus on numbers when they were little, but Bandera said the game had only given him a love of cards and Last said he'd learned to love M&M's because that's what they'd used for chips.

Maybe he wouldn't head over to Mimi's. Tossing the contract into a drawer, he decided to check out the lay of the land. His brothers weren't exactly throwing him a victory party, and they were acting suspicious.

"I'm going to go check the flower bed," he said to the room at large.

No one moved. All the heads stayed down.

Tex shrugged and went out the back door. "Oh, ye of little faith," he said to himself. With excitement, he approached the carefully tended, lovingly prepared, prayerfully watered rose bed that his mother had loved. His own sentimental tribute to her memory.

And found nothing but black, shriveled buds anywhere his bouncing, shocked gaze hit.

Inside the house, the brothers raised their heads to wait.

"Damn it!" Tex yelled. "Crap! Double crap! Fust-a-monkey!"

"Oh, God, it's painful," Navarro said.

"Someone get their gun and put him out of his misery," Bandera pleaded.

"Criminey," Mason said, rubbing his eyes. "I really thought about cutting those things off at the roots and telling him deer had got them. I really did. He would have believed me."

"Well, anything would be better than this!" Fannin exclaimed as the sound of a bucket hitting the wall made them all groan. "He's going out of his mind."

"It'll be worse when he sees that Mimi's roses bloomed just as big as life and twice as beautiful." Last got up from his chair. "I suggest we talk him into doing shots tonight. It's the only way to shut him up. Where's the whiskey? Tequila?"

"If we had neighbors, they would have called the men with straitjackets by now," Crockett observed. "Give me the phone."

"We do have neighbors, but they're used to unholy uproar over here," Calhoun pointed out. "I think the sheriff just turns up the TV a little."

"This time it didn't even get to the Budus Interruptus stage," Last said sadly. "I'd have to regretfully call this Budus No-hope-us."

"Why can't he be normal? Why can't he get that tense over a woman?" Archer demanded. "I could handle him getting that disturbed over a female. But I do find it hard to relate when it's just flowers. God, he's like Ferdinand the bull or something. It's odd, man."

"It's symbolic," Last explained. "It's sexual. Think Georgia O'Keeffe. And it's a memory of our mother, for him. It's the same as us avoiding talking about why we never go hunting Maverick. Why do we avoid it? He could be old. He could be dead. He could be remarried, amnesiac or fill dirt. Dead or alive, damn it, he's somewhere. God only knows every one of us has some kind of phobia, some kind of hang-up. Maybe two. Because we got abandoned and we're pissed. It's not just Tex who wants to throw buckets around and scream frustration. He's just more honest than us. At least his hang-up is harmless. And we make fun of him for it." He took a deep breath. "To make ourselves feel better. And maybe…maybe we should just quit feeling sorry for ourselves."

His brothers stared at him.

"Hell, yeah. I'm finally airing it. I'm talking about *Dad*. Who shoulda been home, hell, twenty freaking years ago."

Dead silence blanketed the room as they stared at the "baby" of the family, the philosopher, the psychologist and even the evangelist, when he got on his spirit pony.

And then, chairs tumbling, M&M's flying and Pokeno cards scattering, the men jumped to their feet to find someplace else to be other than with the truth.

IN HER GARDEN, MIMI HEARD the roar of disappointment and pulled her gloves off with a sigh. "That would be Tex," she murmured. "And I bet myself a buck he gets no sympathy from his brothers."

She tossed her gloves into the rose garden and began walking toward the ranch house next door. It took her five minutes, but that would give him time to pull himself together. The sound of something like a mower or a Weed-Eater made her walk faster.

Heading to the back of the house, she found Tex, Weed-Eater in hand, destroying his rosebushes. Pieces of leaves and stems flew as he worked a mighty hatchet job—as far down to the ground as he could get.

"Tex!" she shouted. "Tex!"

He glanced at her and switched the thing off reluctantly. "Hi, Mimi."

"Um, Tex," she began, "hey, congratulations. I heard about your awesome ride."

"Thanks."

Neither of them glanced toward his handiwork.

"I heard your dad stabilized," he said.

"For the moment." She stared into his beautiful dark eyes, so much like Mason's. All the brothers had them. They pulled a woman in and kept her captive.

She knew that firsthand. "Sorry about your roses," she finally said.

"It's not just the roses," he said after glancing wildly around. "It's something more than that."

She nodded. "You know, you're one of the best of the bunch, Tex," she said.

He looked at her. "I don't feel like it."

"Well, you are."

They were silent for a moment. "Hey, I hear you might be expecting."

"I hope so. I'll know for certain next week."

"That's great. I'll be an uncle." He smiled for the first time.

"Yeah. And I'll be a mother."

"Hey, how weird is that?" He grinned at her, and she smiled back.

"Extra-weird," she said, and they both laughed together. Then she grew serious. "Brian doesn't know yet."

He looked at her.

"I'm waiting for a special time to tell him," she hedged. "It's all been so crazy and fast since Dad's been in the hospital. There just hasn't been the proper moment."

"But you told Mason."

She nodded. "Habit. I've been telling Mason things for years. He was the only person I talked to about stuff. Just keep this under your hat for now, okay?"

He looked back at the rose stalks that the Weed-Eater had chewed on but not destroyed. "Sure, Mimi. You'll get it all worked out."

"Tex, listen, I think the problem you're having is that you need new bushes. I think your pilot program of using similar plants to what your mom had may not be right for you. Have you ever thought of that?"

"Um, no."

He didn't want to, she knew. He wanted everything the way his mother had loved it.

"Well, change can be good. Sometimes."

They smiled again. "Thanks, Mimi," he said. "By the way, can I give you something to give to Brian?"

"Sure."

"Great. Come on in the house for a second, if you don't mind, and I'll get it."

She followed him in, automatically glancing around for Mason. "I'll wait right here," she said, settling into the armchair in front of the TV. "I've always wondered what it felt like to kick back like this."

"Here." Tex put the recliner all the way back.

"Now, close your eyes, little mama, and rest. I'll be right back."

She did, and the leather felt good. Maybe she should get one of these for Brian, she thought, for their first anniversary. No, better yet, it could be his Dad gift when she told him that they were expecting.

Hopefully it would be a pleasant surprise.

MASON STARED DOWN AT THE woman asleep in his recliner. Who would ever have thought his little hell-belle could look so sweet? Normally, he shared his armchair begrudgingly, but he kinda liked her being in it. It made him feel...sort of protective of her. Possessive, even.

Oh, boy. He couldn't feel that way about another man's wife. Tearing his gaze away from her, he focused on his brother. Tex sat beside her, watching the TV on Mute. "Is she okay?" Mason asked his brother.

"I think she's found her just-right chair," Tex said without looking up. "She's probably tired from being, you know...pregnant."

Mason's gaze popped to his brother. "Did she tell you it was for certain?"

Tex shrugged. "Guess she has reason to be positive or she wouldn't have mentioned it to us. By the way, we're not supposed to buy Brian a cigar or anything. She hasn't told him."

Mason frowned. "Because?"

"Because she's waiting for the just-right moment."

That seemed reasonable. "Are you okay?" Mason asked.

Tex glanced at him. "Why wouldn't I be?"

Whew, he wasn't going there if Tex didn't want to. "No special reason," Mason said, thinking, well, hell, maybe the great Weed-Eater massacre is a clue that you might not have been just fine-'n'-dandy. "So, when's Sleeping Beauty surrendering my chair?"

"Don't know. How long does a pregnant woman nap?"

"I don't even know how long a not-pregnant woman naps."

Tex squinted at the TV. "Guess we're going to learn a lot of things we never knew before, if Mimi's got a bun in the oven. How do you feel about that, anyway?"

"Fine. It's all fine," Mason said. "Looking forward to teaching it how to play football."

"It?"

"Boy or girl, it doesn't matter. It's going out for forward passes so that I can finally play football. I never really had time with this crew." Yeah, a hell of an admission. But he'd worked his ass off being the father figure, and keeping eleven boys in hand didn't allow for much time to be a friend.

Mimi awakened, stretching and looking at them with a smile. "Hey, Mason," she said, her voice soft from sleepiness. "Did I steal your chair?"

"It's fine," he repeated hurriedly. He couldn't say he was in a hurry for her to leave now that she was awake and he was staring into her blue eyes, but something was definitely moving in his jeans that shouldn't be. Her braid was shoved through a base-ball cap. She was wearing cropped jeans and a short-sleeved blue sweater. Little white mule tennies on her feet revealed shapely ankles he'd never noticed before.

Oh, Lord, he didn't want to end up like Tex, stark raving mad over something he was never going to get over. Mimi Interruptus.

"Tex, did you want to show me something? I didn't mean to doze off on you."

"Yeah." He handed her Cissy's contract, giving Mason a chance to walk off the tension. "Can you ask Brian if he minds going over this contract to look for loopholes in the fine print? I'm trying to get Cissy Kisserton out of her contract." Mimi's eyes lit on him, and he hurried to dig out. "For Hannah. Hannah asked me to check into things."

"Oh." Mimi nodded and glanced down at the con-tract.

The men went back to watching the mute TV; Tex could feel the back of his neck burn red. Was it wrong to do a favor for one's friends, he asked him-self? He looked after Mimi. He looked after Cissy. It was all the same.

"Well, there's a big fat loophole right here on page one," Mimi said, grabbing his attention. "I don't know if you noticed or not, but it says right here on page one that if Cissy marries, she's out of a job."

"Huh?" Tex said. "She was married when she was hired by Marvella, though she didn't tell."

"And probably that's why she didn't care about the proviso being in here," Mimi said. "Is she still married?"

"No," Tex said, his head swimming. "You mean, all she has to do to null and void this sucker is say I do?"

"I think so. It says right here that her employment terminates if she becomes married, pregnant or physically challenged. I think that decodes to mean ugly." Mimi laughed. "Marvella is not an equal opportunity employer. I think that would get her in trouble with the EEOC."

Mason and Tex looked at each other.

"Hell, Tex," Mason said, "all you have to do to save Cissy is marry her, get her pregnant or fatten her up and cut a Mohawk out of that platinum hair. Talk her into a nose ring."

"She could start eating onions so her breath is always bad, and she could wear black fingernail polish," Mimi suggested, feeding off of Mason.

"She could become a *man,*" Mason said slyly.

Mimi and Mason went off into the giggles of their days before everything had gone wrong, but Tex was too busy pondering to care.

Marriage. Pregnancy. Or a midlife crisis complete with Oprah and buckets of ice cream and maybe sprouting armpit hair.

No, Cissy was too fastidious to let herself go. And she had nine kids, so that let out the pregnancy route.

That left one option, and it was so numbing and incredible that he almost couldn't even consider it.

On the other hand, it made a strange sort of sense.

CISSY ENDURED THE HATEFUL looks as she walked
into the dining room of the Never Lonely Cut-n-
Gurls. Cissy was Enemy number 1—but maybe in
her heart she wanted to be.

She had wanted Tex to win. And she'd deliber-
ately talked Marvella out of buying him at the raffle.
After having a long heart-to-heart talk with herself,
she knew that it was time for her to face facts. And
it also meant bucking up. No more praying for a way
out. There was about a year left on her contract, not
a lifetime.

"Cissy," Marvella said, "you're looking simply
horrible today, dear."

The stylists laughed.

"Are we pining for something? Someone?" Marvella asked.

"No." Cissy put her plate down on the table.
"You can all resume eating," she said to her sisters.
"Although my gran always said that loose lips sink
ships, so you all might want to tighten up on the
starboard sides. And the port sides."

Okay, so now open battle had been declared.

"Witch!" someone whispered under her breath so
that Cissy could hear.

"Maybe," she replied calmly. "But you look like
you've already had the evil eye liberally applied to
you, so I'll pass you over today."

Marvella thumped her fork down, glaring at Cissy.
"Why did you do it?"

"I didn't know Tex would win. No one has stayed
on Bloodthirsty before."

"You know how I feel about my sister," Marvella stated.

Cissy thought about how she'd give everything she owned to have her brother and two sisters back. "And I think that's a shame. Maybe you should make up. Forgive her. Life is short, Marvella."

So many women at the table sucked in their breaths Cissy feared she was going to have to perform the Heimlich on someone. "Easy, girls," she said, "chew before you choke."

Marvella seemed to have turned into a frozen sculpture at the head of the table. "After everything I've done for you," she said. "Those ratty kids of yours would have had nothing without me. How did you think you were going to feed them? Did you think *Granny* was going to be able to lift her share of the load? Did you dream that looking like an expensive hooker was going to land you a job in some *secretary's* office?"

"Marvella, I am sorry that you're upset," Cissy said, "but it's a charity rodeo. It's not a windfall inheritance. It's not life and death. You have a problem with anger management, and frankly, it's not your best asset."

The table went completely silent as Marvella and Cissy stared each other down like dueling foes.

"I will never terminate your contract," Marvella promised her with a voice of steel. "I don't care what happens to those brats or that old woman you call Gran. And if she should croak while you're in my employ, you will not be attending her funeral."

"You can't do that. It's not within your rights as an employer," Cissy said.

"First of all, read your contract with a fine eye, honey. I own you. And for the amount of money I sent to your family, you should be grateful. But you're not…and you know, I've just decided you're going to have to take a major pay cut." She smiled icily at Cissy. "Bad economy, you know. Downsizing. Scaling back. And here's a fresh twist," she said, glancing around the table, "I'll split your pay cut between the first three women who make your life so miserable that you apologize to me."

Cissy stared blankly at her employer. "You're a bitch."

"Well, that really hurts my feelings." Marvella smiled and rose from her chair like a queen. "Good night, ladies. Have at it." She gestured regally to Cissy and left the dining room.

The stylists turned their gazes to Cissy, looking like so many hungry cats.

Chapter Nine

Cissy had found her spine, and all in all, she felt better about her situation. At least until she opened her bedroom door and realized someone was in her room.

"Cissy!" Tex said quietly, but loud enough to get her attention. "It's only me."

Sighing with relief, she went inside and locked the door behind her. "Have you ever thought about calling?"

"Have you ever considered not being so jumpy?"

"No. Marvella's put a bounty on me, and I thought one of the stylists was trying to collect." She shrugged at Tex. "It's just drama."

He commandeered the chair in front of the window and looked out. "Bad thing, drama."

"It's okay. I'll survive it." She wasn't so sure, but it didn't matter anymore. She had just about given up hope of ever escaping Marvella's endless hatred.

"I'd offer to stay and protect you," Tex said.

"That's heroic. But I'm not your problem."

"Well, you sort of are. You've become my problem, anyway, because we keep rescuing each other and that creates ties and, you know, it's sort of there between us.''

She looked at him. ''What's between us?''

''Who knows?'' He tipped the chair and grinned at her. ''Something usually reserved for soap operas, probably. What do you say we find out?''

''What are you talking about?'' He looked way too sexy shoved back in that chair. Right now, she was almost depressed enough to tell him that she needed his lips to kiss away the fear and desolation building inside her.

''Mimi found a clause in your contract we think we can use,'' Tex said. ''But sit in my lap while you try it on because I have to whisper it to you.''

She glared at him, tempted and determined not to show it. ''I don't think so.''

''Didn't you say that your stylist pals have incentive to do you harm?''

She nodded.

''Well, I'm watching the street here, and they're lining up out there, babe.''

She flew to the window.

''Looks to me like they're planning to call attention to you.''

Three stylists held up signs that she could read. ''Cissy is a Sissy,'' she said. ''Cissy Gives Bad Kissy. Cissy Takes a Pi—''

''That one refers to the fact that you're really a man in drag,'' Tex interrupted. ''No further clarification needed.''

She gasped. ''How dare they?''

''You said—''

"I know what I said! But I didn't think they'd take it into the town!"

He sat her in his lap, and she went without protesting. "Why would you imagine Marvella's girls wouldn't be creative?"

"I don't know. I was thinking garden snakes and things. That's what they did before."

"Well, the ante is obviously upped."

"Back to the clause you want me to try on," Cissy said, a bit desperately.

He grinned. "That's my brave girl. Now, listen carefully, because the choice you make will affect your future. Really."

She couldn't tell if he was serious. Outside, she could hear the chanting stylists. "Tex, if you truly have a way to rescue me, now's the time to hit me with it."

"Wish granted," he said cheerfully. "You need to be ugly."

Her mouth opened helplessly.

"Well, now, if that's not a sight for sore eyes." Tex looked inside her mouth. "Very pink tongue. Very sexy."

She snapped her mouth shut before saying, "You mean like stop washing my hair? Don't brush my teeth?"

"You have to be physically challenged. Yeah, that probably fits. It's shallow to say that you should stop at going bald, because I know very attractive bald women. And major weight gain won't help much, either, if you've been looking at the recent lingerie shows for booty-full ladies. A lot of men find meat instead of bones very attractive. I'd opt for all of the above and see if you can hit any of Marvella's deal-breakers."

"Let me see if I understand you. You want me to gain a hell of a lot of weight, shave my hair, oil my head and grow grunge on my teeth."

"That would definitely put a crimp in my get-along," he said, too cheerfully for her temper.

"Do you have a plan B?" she demanded. "Because I'm not certain I can meet all of those criteria. Why should I give myself a cavity over a crazy woman?"

"Well, you probably shouldn't. Okay, plan B involves pregnancy."

She wanted to slap him. "You're toying with a situation that is crucial to me."

"I'm being crucial! Didn't you read your contract?"

"Actually, yes. And I never saw anything about being physically challenged *or* pregnant. I wouldn't have signed that."

Tex narrowed his gaze on her. "When you gave me the contract, you didn't refresh your memory by glancing over it?"

"No. I was in a huge hurry to get out of her office before I got caught."

"Is there any way your signature could have been forged?"

She shrugged. "At this point, what difference would that make? I can't prove that's not my contract."

"True. So we're back to getting you pregnant."

"Oh, no, we're not," Cissy said. "I can't feed the many mouths I have now."

"So true."

She sighed, wishing he hadn't gotten her all excited about nothing. "Tex, is it too much to hope that you have a plan C? And that it's a real plan?"

"There is a plan C," he said, and she could tell he was very reluctant, "but the other two are much easier."

"I think we'd best at least discuss the third option. The first two don't exactly get my hopes up."

"Marriage," he said simply.

"Marriage?" she repeated. "I've been married. I didn't enjoy it."

"That reminds me. Did Marvella know you were? I mean, obviously, she didn't."

"I never mentioned it. When I came here, I didn't know what had happened to my husband. One day, he was in his house, and then he was gone. And after a while, I called the police, and then I realized he was never coming back. Frankly, I thought it more likely that he'd found another woman. It never occurred to me, given our circumstances, that he might have been killed. Seemed more likely that he'd tired of our marriage of convenience."

"Well, Marvella has no use for you if you're married."

"I have no use for being married."

"But it gets you out of the contract," he pointed out.

"Yes, but then I'm right back where I was before.

I'd like my life to go forward. Not back into the pits.''

"I'm not suggesting you marry another gangster, Cissy.''

She looked at him, her gaze connecting with his as she realized he was finally being serious.

Tex took a deep breath. "I'm suggesting you marry *me*.''

The look on Cissy's face was priceless. Thank God he hadn't had too much invested in the offer, or he'd be devastated. She looked like she'd just as soon become high priestess of the snake species.

"Okay,'' she said brightly. "So we're back to me losing my toothbrush. Maybe I could go retro punk rock instead of totally bald. That might be even more effective—''

"No, all the men who love kink would be after you, and the girls would be jealous and try to copy you, and then this would become the Never Lonely Cut-n-Kinks, and it would be superdisturbing. Trust me.''

"It's so sad that I've come to a place in my life where yet another man offers to marry me to bail me out.'' She looked at him with soft eyes. "I suppose you don't want to sleep with me again, either. That time in the barn was a one-off.''

"Now that you mention it—''

"I really don't want another marriage of convenience, even though you're a nice guy and cute and smell good and can ride bulls just for the hell of it. Do you know what I mean? There's *marriage*, and then's there's marriage, and the next time I do it, I really, really want it to be for real.''

His Adam's apple jumped in his throat. What could he say? Of course he wanted to sleep with her! He didn't know what kind of weirdo her husband had been, but Tex recognized a superhot, asteroidal kind of woman when he saw one. They were as rare as comets, but this woman was Cissy's Comet. He'd be happy to catch onto her tail and ride all around the galaxy. Right now, just from her sitting on his lap, he had a hard-on he was trying to camouflage.

But he couldn't say that. Could he? It seemed ungentlemanly when he was supposed to be rescuing her. *Yes, Cissy, I'll marry you to get you out of your contract, and you'll have sex with me because I'm an opportunistic pig.*

''We could see what developed,'' he said hopefully, trying to hedge.

She shook her head. ''You're awfully kind to bail me out. We've done that a lot for each other. But I really want true love. It's the pits when the moving vans come and the utilities get shut off and your house goes back to the bank because you're breaking off what shouldn't have been in the first place.''

Tex drummed his fingers on the windowsill. ''We could agree it would only be for a short time, but long enough so that Marvella realizes you're safe from anything she might decide to do.''

''Another contract,'' Cissy said softly. ''Yet another deal. Do you know, Tex, I just don't think I can go into another thing in my life that's brokered up front.''

"Cissy, there's no guarantee on happiness, and there's no forever. I know what I'm talking about here. You've got reasons to consider my offer." Outside, the evil stylist stepsisters had gone quiet. "They're not going to give you peace for long."

"I can handle it."

"Do you really want to apologize to Marvella?" He thought he might as well illuminate the dark side of her situation.

"No, I don't. The very thought makes me shudder."

"Then be a kick-ass female with a trashy side," he told her. "Let's do the unexpected. She's got you right where she wants you. A prisoner. And it only goes down from here, unless you get out."

She bowed her head before looking at him with those deep aquamarine eyes highlighted by the silver fall of hair. "Just what would you get out of this?"

Ah, the trap. She didn't want another marriage of convenience; she didn't want another "deal." Check it out: she *did* want to be made love to. He wasn't about to admit that marrying her would give him an instant bravo from his family. Goodbye Budus Interruptus, forever. Because nobody could look at this female and assume he wasn't doing everything possible to keep her. Pulling out all the emotional stops, diving in way past the superficial Tex. And stay away from the rescue theme, he told himself, she'll toss you out for that one, too, because she wants to do this on her own.

Not if I can help it, he thought.

"I get safety," he said. "Safety from all the

women who chase me. It does get irritating when females tirelessly chase a man.'' He didn't need to elaborate. He'd just been won by ten eager ladies—she could draw her own conclusions about his truthfulness. ''And I get *you*,'' he said diplomatically. ''I think I'd like to have you around for, oh, three months or so.''

''As friends?'' she asked.

''If you like,'' he said gallantly, but the real answer was Hell, no!

''If I agree to this marriage, Tex, we'll have to change that,'' she said, her voice so hopeful it sent velvet thrills all over his skin. ''I'd really like you to make love to me again. Not a rush-of-passion thing. I want one night under the stars.''

''Well, we'll see,'' he said magnanimously, not wanting to scare her half to death and not wanting to appear too eager. ''Friends is fine, too,'' he lied.

''I'd like this marriage to be real,'' she said, her smile shy.

''Sure, sure,'' he said, open to agreement. Where sex was concerned, he was going to be very easy.

She curled gentle fingers into the hair at the nape of his neck, lightly stroking against his skin. ''I won't know much about lovemaking. You'll have to show me.''

His eyes closed as he enjoyed her fingertips touching and feeling him. ''You knew everything you needed to know when we were in the barn.''

Cissy said. ''That only took a few minutes. We didn't want anyone to catch us. I'm talking about *real* lovemaking.''

"We can be in a bed next time."

"It's more than just location. It's taking time, and depth of emotion, and learning how to please a man."

"But—"

"Tex," she said patiently. "I lived with my grandmother and nine children. Even before my family went to South America, there was a lot of work to be done. What do you expect? That I was out every night at the bar picking up the regulars? My brother would have killed any man who touched me."

She looked at him with a soft smile, seeing that he didn't understand. "That time in the barn was my first."

He sat straight up, confusion running through him. Healthy male fear. Curiosity. Total extreme sexual juggernaut fireballing along his every nerve. "You were a virgin?"

"Yes."

He shook his head dumbly. "I would have known."

"How? We were moving so fast that I lost my Make My Day panties in the straw and had to go back the next day to retrieve them. It's not like we took the time to exchange much more than our names."

"Why didn't you tell me then?"

"I didn't want you to know. You wouldn't have made love to me if you'd known the truth."

"Why? Why would you have done it with me?"

She sighed. "You were there."

That wasn't exactly what he wanted to hear. "I was *there?*"

"Well, yes. You wanted me, and I wanted to be wanted for a change."

"Cissy, all men want you. Sex drives go into load-and-lock when you're around."

She shrugged. "I liked the way you intended to cover for Laredo. I thought that was very sexy. Loyalty means a lot to me. And your brothers are good men. Ornery and a bit rough, but good. But also, I could tell you were the kind of man who would love me and leave me. And with my situation with Marvella, I couldn't have any romantic entanglements."

"But…" It wasn't supposed to happen this way. If they were agreeing to a marriage that lasted more than twenty-four hours, he was entitled to sex. Any man would agree. But if he'd been her first lover, that was special. Virginity went hand in hand with commitment—and that was almost a deal-breaker. Neither of them professed to want a long-term thing. The bargain: she got out of her contract; he got Last and all of Malfunction Junction off his neck about his intimacy issues. And then they went their separate ways. Yet how could he love her and then leave her after knowing the truth?

No way was he touching her now that he realized he had a bona fide good girl on his hands. "Uh—"

She laid fingertips against his lips. "Aren't you always claiming to like trashy girls? Can't you give just a little on the trashiness? I can be that, if you'll let me."

She was still confused about his definition of

trashy, but because she'd replaced her fingertips on his mouth with her lips, and was kissing him as if their tongues were doing the slip-'n'-slide and their mouths were suction cups, he lost all of his concentration and slid his arms around her. There was no hiding his full-on arousal now. He wanted her, he wanted her bad, and he wanted her now.

And then she was away from him, her lips miraculously absent from his face where they belonged. "Whew," he said, "if you were a virgin, where'd you learn to kiss like that?"

She laughed. "If a girl's going to stay a virgin, then she better be a damn good kisser or she'll *never* get a date."

And then she ran her fingers through the ends of his hair just the way he was deciding he liked. With a giggle and a kiss, she'd gone over to the trashy side all on her own. She was tricky. Minx appeal. A little bit bad girl.

That scared him more than anything. Exactly what kind of deal was he getting himself into?

Chapter Ten

"And then again," Tex said, "maybe a pretend engagement would suffice. You think?"

She looked at him, and he wondered if he'd ever seen a more beautiful woman. Whether he wanted to be honest with himself or not, Cissy frightened him out of his wits. What he wanted to do was steal her, take her off to a cabin in the woods, make love to her for at least a week and see if he could get her out of his system.

She got up to brush her hair, and everything went to black in his brain.

"I'm thinking it's got to be marriage." Her eyes met his in the mirror. "But it's a pretty big favor, Tex. I'm not so certain that it's not too much to ask of a friend."

He swallowed hard. "Well, friends help each other out." And he meant that. They were going to be nothing but friends, so the parting would be easy. "Where should we do it?"

She turned. "Do what?"

His breath was coming more shallow as he thought

about sex, and marriage, and sex again. "Get married."

"The courthouse?"

"Too close for comfort. If I'm rescuing you, I plan on getting you far away from Marvella."

"If you get me to Jellyfish's riverboat, I can work there," she pointed out. "I know he would like to have me hostess in his casino again."

That was true. And Hannah would approve. "Of course, Malfunction Junction would be pretty safe. My brothers wouldn't put up with anybody coming around trying to make trouble, and Marvella did follow you to Jellyfish's riverboat."

"That's when I was still under contract. We're going to leave a note saying that the damage is done."

He grinned at that. "The damage. Yeah. I like that."

She smiled a bit shyly. "Not that it's for real or anything, but getting married on the riverboat would be a wedding dream come true for me. It sounds so romantic and peaceful and close to heaven."

Her eyes softened, and his heart melted. The itch to make her dreams come true was strong. "Then again, there's got to be a quickie drive-through place somewhere. I know they do them in Nevada. We'd be safe doing that, because Marvella would never think of it, and it'd be fast, like ordering a McDonald's Happy Meal for the kids, and it'd be unsentimental. Like, over, done, Roger, out."

Her smile slipped away. "Very efficient and business-like."

He nodded, telling himself that he was right to

keep their mission from slipping over into romance. It was what they both wanted.

Of course, it stunk to be the horse's ass instead of the hero.

The phone rang, and Cissy picked it up. "Hello?"

The line disconnected. The phone rang again. She picked it up again. "Hello?"

The line disconnected.

This went on several more times. "I'm getting worried that it might be Gran, and the line isn't holding," Cissy said.

"Just a minute. Keep answering." Tex went out the door stealthily. Watching carefully, he made his way downstairs to where he could see into the lobby. At the receptionist's desk, Valentine was dialing numbers, listening, then hanging up. Over and over again. He grinned and crept up behind her. "Hey!"

She screamed and dropped the handset.

"Cissy's not in her room," he said. "Do you know where she is? I need to thank her for baking me those cookies."

Valentine's eyes were huge from her fright. "Cookies?"

"Yeah. Think they had laxatives in them, but I've got innards made of leather." He thumped his stomach. "I think she wanted me to lose," he said conspiratorially.

"Lose?"

He shrugged. "What do you think?"

She shook her head.

"Well, just goes to show you that some things are not what they seem." He grinned at her and headed back upstairs with a wink. "Pack up," he told Cissy when he was back in her room. "Tell me what you want help with."

She pulled out her silver-foil luggage, tossing it on the bed. "The phone quit ringing."

"Yeah, but the whistle is being blown on you, so let's pack fast."

Cissy piled clothes and personal things into her bag. She didn't have a lot in her room, and she was economical with her motions. The last thing she packed was the photo of her family, surrounding it with soft clothes before she zipped the bag. "Why now?"

"Because they're going to make your life miserable. And I want Marvella to know you left with me. She'll be a lot less inclined to make trouble for you this time. If she decides to give chase, we'll already be married. Under the circumstances, I think it's best if we go hunt up Hawk and have him perform one of those Native American ceremonies he performed on Ranger and Hannah. Worked for them."

He scribbled a quick note and left it on the mirror.

"What does it say?" Cissy asked.

"'Dear Marvella, I'm Cissy Jefferson now. Put that in your pipe and smoke it,'" he read. "This is not going to be a popular manifesto."

She giggled. "It's not true yet."

He grabbed her luggage. "Come on. I can't quibble semantics. You know my intentions are good."

They hurried down the stairs and ran past Valentine. Tex gave her a wave. "I found her! Thanks, Valentine!"

Valentine's jaw dropped. She picked up the phone, punching numbers swiftly. Tex reached over and took it from her. "Never mind. I'll tell her myself. Marvella?" he said when she answered. "This is Tex Jefferson. I just wanted to tell you that you'll never be the woman your sister is. It's time to accept that fact and move on." He handed the phone back to Valentine. "You can talk to her now."

And then he grabbed Cissy's hand and ran with her to his truck. He opened the door and helped her inside.

"I feel like a runaway bride!"

He laughed and kissed her on the nose. "Let's go get you married. I want to make certain this thing is all tied up nice and legal for the time we're going to be together."

"Remember your promise," she said. "About the one night of real lovemaking under the stars. Romance. All the honeymoon wonderland that real couples get."

The grin fled his face. "Escape first, and then details."

CISSY GLANCED OVER AT TEX. He was quiet and had been ever since they'd left Lonely Hearts Station. He'd called Archer once for directions to Hawk's place, since she couldn't remember exactly how to get there—Ranger rolling down the embankment wasn't exactly an address code; there were lots of embankments, after all—and those were the only words Tex had spoken. Of course, he was concentrating on driving fast down the open highway. But there was one thing she hadn't told him.

"Tex?" she said.

"Yeah?"

He didn't seem open to light conversation, so she figured it was best to say what was on her mind. "There is one detour we have to make."

"You need a ladies'?" he asked. "We got enough of a head start on Marvella that I don't think that'll be a problem. Just don't stop to powder your nose, too."

"No, not that. Tex, before we go to Hawk's, we need to go to Gran's."

For a moment, he didn't say much. "Well, we're in a hurry."

"I know. But while I may be able to pull this trick on Marvella, I can't marry you without my grandmother meeting you. She wouldn't understand at all."

She could almost hear his heart beating.

"All right," he said slowly. "Detour, it is. Tell me how to get there."

She told him the directions, and he nodded. But he didn't say anything else. Her heart sank. She didn't need his silence to know that he wouldn't want the complication of meeting her family. It wasn't Marvella—Gran's was the last place Marvella would look because she would automatically assume Cissy wouldn't go someplace so obvious. No, meeting family meant explaining everything to Gran. And while it was easy enough for Tex to marry Cissy knowing they'd soon divorce, she knew it would be hard for him to look her grandmother in the eye and admit that he wouldn't be Cissy's husband for very long. And he certainly didn't want more family issues; he had enough of his own. "Tex," she said again. "You'll like Gran."

"I know I will."

And that was all he said.

TOO SOON, THEY WERE AT Gran's house, the home where Cissy was raised. Tex would never have imagined the place to be so peaceful and tranquil. It was a tiny house, maybe what one would call "gingerbread style." Delicate and fragile. Spring flowers bloomed on the porch in pots, and children's chalk drawings colored the sidewalk out front. A banner with a ladybug on it hung from a flagpole near the door. An elderly woman came out on the porch and waved at them.

"Gran!" Cissy exclaimed, running up the sidewalk in the high heels, skirt and feminine blouse she'd changed into in the truck. She had wanted to look nice to go home, and he had to admit the effort had paid off spectacularly.

She looked as if she'd been working at an office, and suddenly, Tex realized what Cissy might have been, if life hadn't thrown her so many curves. The old woman was engulfed in her tall granddaughter's hug, and all kinds of children came tearing out the screen door to envelop Cissy and Gran in hugs of their own.

It was the kind of reunion Tex and his brothers had always silently dreamed of and knew would never happen for them. There had been no pastel chalk drawings after their parents were gone. And yet, they'd been a family.

A rough one, in contrast to this one.

Cissy couldn't stop kissing little faces, and slowly Tex got out of his truck. He watched her eat them up as if she'd never get to hold them long enough, and he began to shake inside. Gran saw him approach, her large aquamarine eyes—just like Cissy's—watching him with interest.

He felt like a coward.

"Hi, Tex," she said simply.

"Hi, Gran," he replied.

And she engulfed him in a hug just like the one she'd given Cissy, only on him her hug ended about chest high.

His nervousness evaporated. In its place, he felt a soothing sense of family. From inside, the scent of cookies wafted onto the spring breeze. He sighed, letting all the warmth of family flow over him.

Something tugged on his jeans pocket, and he glanced down into the face of a sandy-haired child. "Howdy," he said.

"Who are you?" the child asked. Her siblings and cousins awaited his response, staring at him as if they'd never seen a man.

Or a father figure. "I'm Tex. I'm—" He stopped. He didn't know what Cissy was going to tell her family.

"You're a cowboy," one of the boys said.

"That's right. I'm a cowboy."

"Aunt Cissy's never brought home a cowboy before," the little boy said.

"She's never brought home any man," the eldest girl said, her eyes wide. "Are you going to marry her?"

Tex cleared his throat, looking to *Aunt* Cissy for help. Gran seemed just as interested in the answer as the children.

Cissy smiled at him, her gaze understanding.
"Let's show Mr. Tex inside. We don't want to over-
whelm him immediately."

Too late. He already was.

AFTER A LUNCH OF GRILLED cheese sandwiches—the
childrens' favorite—carrot sticks (run through something that made them wavy), pickles (had to be mini
dill sticks) and fruit (strawberries and grapes cleaned
by Cissy), Cissy and Tex headed for Hawk's palace
in the wooded hills.

"So," Cissy said as Tex turned up onto the highway. "Shaking in your boots?"

"Pretty much. Cute kids."

Yeah, she figured they were pretty scary to him.
"Gran liked you."

"I liked her, too."

Conversation was not ebbing and flowing. It was
coming to a dead stop. "Tex, you don't have to do
this."

"I'm shaken but not deterred," he told her. "You
just better decide if this is what you want to do."

Now that they were within a couple of hours of
meeting up with Hawk, she had begun to think her
situation through more thoroughly. She hadn't told
the children she and Tex were going to get married
because she didn't want them to be disappointed
when she and Tex divorced. Gran had been let in on
the secret, and she'd given Tex a warm hug and
thanked him for helping them.

He'd gruffly replied that it was nothing.

To which Gran had answered that, to her and the
children, it was everything.

The spirit in her tone seemed to have surprised Tex. Truthfully, Cissy and Gran were weighed under with too many things they couldn't handle. They were relieved to have someone provide a way out.

And Gran hadn't asked why Tex was marrying Cissy for three months, but Cissy had told Gran that he was escaping some family issues. Because of his father's abandonment, Tex wanted an anchor to help settle him. Marriage would do that.

Wouldn't it? "Maybe a pretend engagement would be better," Cissy said. "Then there's no messy paperwork later. We just say goodbye to each other." She looked at him, but he was focused on the road.

"I don't think Hawk performs pretend engagement ceremonies," he finally said. "It's best if we cover our bases, and then my family will shut up, and Marvella will give up."

"Okay," she said with a sigh. "If you insist."

"That doesn't sound very bridelike."

"I don't mean to sound ungrateful. And I'm not asking for perfection…" It was hard to say what was bothering her. Leaving the children behind hurt. A second marriage of convenience wasn't something she was proud of. But then, she wouldn't have wanted a real marriage—at least not with Tex. She had sensed how awkward he was with her children.

You couldn't make a man want a ready-made family when he was from a large family that drove him crazy. "After we get married, there's no rule that we have to stay together every second, is there?"

He glanced at her. "What do you mean?"

"Well, we're only doing this for surface reasons."

"Don't say that! At least never say it around my brothers. That *surface* word will let the secret out of the shade. Don't say *superficial, temporary, convenience,* or *artificial.*"

"Artificial?"

"I don't know. I just threw that in there because I was thinking of artificial insemination."

Her brows rose. "Do you think of that often?"

"I don't know why it went through my mind. Substitute fake for artificial, and add it to the list."

"So you won't mind if I live at the riverboat, then, without you. That way I can't make any slip-ups. And you can go back to the ranch. I know you're needed there."

"Is that what you want?"

She shrugged. "There's no need for you to baby-sit me. I'll be a safe, married woman."

He frowned. "I don't know. Let's talk about it later."

She could tell he was rattled. And grouchy. "Tex, you were not just artificially inseminated with nine children. You don't have to be their father."

Flipping the radio on, he said, "I need to think. And I think best if I'm not talking."

Chapter Eleven

Tex had a long time to think on the way to Hawk's place. He added up a list of pros and cons in his head. Pluses and minuses to what he was about to do.

None of it was a plus or a minus completely. More like multiplication. Tex times ten.

Gran, for instance. Definitely a family complication. But she had roped him in when she'd treated him as if he was already part of her big, happy, cozy world. The hug had stolen his heart. And, she'd watched him with big eyes that didn't judge. She accepted him, and that was real new.

Even when he slipped her money that she didn't want to accept, all he had to do was explain that he had eleven brothers, and that Mason had raised them all. That only now was Tex beginning to appreciate what his brother had gone through to keep them all together and out of foster homes, as the good people of Union Junction had believed was best. Mason had put a very stubborn boot in that idea and kept the siblings together instead. And whether any of them wanted to admit it or not, they were damn glad, and lucky for it. "I'm marrying Cissy," he'd told Gran, "and she's helping me, in a way that matters a lot to me. So I want to help her family. Because I know how hard it is to do it alone."

Nodding, Gran had taken the money, said thank you and hugged him in that special warm way she had.

So she was more plus than minus. Drat.

Okay. Nine kids, he reminded himself. Nine! Nine ragtag little minuses. Loved and well behaved, of course, but the evidence of living tightly was everywhere, from the patched clothes to the worn rugs. He swallowed. Those nine minuses didn't know if their parents were ever returning, and he could totally relate to that.

Thing was, it really sucked when a child didn't know what was going to happen. The worst, though, was when the child woke up one day and knew his dreams were shattered forever. It had made him and his brothers wild and, yes, damn it, somewhat emotionally stunted.

Something inside him wanted better for those kids. He wanted to make their pain go away.

Time to put away the plus-and-minus debate. It obviously wasn't going to get him anywhere. "Sorry I'm not good company."

"That's okay. You're not here for my entertainment." She serenely turned the pages of a magazine, reading over recipes. "Do you like homemade chicken pot pie?"

He gulped, the vision of Cissy in stiletto heels and nothing more than a frilly white pinafore tied just above her ass almost too much to bear. "I never turn down a good meal."

"Do you ever cook?"

"No. Too busy. Learning to tolerate sauerkraut, though. Helga cooks lots of German food." He frowned. "But I could go for Japanese, you know. Or Mexican. Or even soul food. Mm-mm! Cajun," he murmured hungrily. "A housekeeper with a talent for Italian would be awesome. But just when I think we've talked Mason into giving Helga up, he waffles. I believe that's Belgian, not German, by the way, and we don't get those. We get some potato pancake thing sometimes. He does waffle, though."

"Why? Does he like her cooking?"

"I don't know. She takes real good care of him." Cissy turned a page. "And you?"

"I won't let her. Mason's the needy one."

Cissy laughed. "No."

"No, what?"

"No, he's not. Not like you are. He's on his own, except for the cooking, which is to be expected. He can't do it all."

He could feel his temper gauge rise. "I am not needy."

"Are you going to want a traditional wife for three months?" she asked, looking up at him at the same time he glanced at her.

He jerked his gaze back to the road. "Uh—" Was she talking about homemade chicken pot pies or sex? No, they'd agreed to one night of real romance, and nothing other than that. So it was the pies. "Are you offering to cook for me?"

"Are you offering to cook for *me?*"

Shaking his head, he said, "Nah. I'll buy the groceries if you cook the food."

"You have to eat without complaining. Not like you do for poor Helga."

"Poor Helga?" He chuckled. "Helga's strict, believe me."

"But she takes total care of Mason. So is that what you want from me? Or are we going our separate ways until the divorce?"

He squinted. "I haven't thought that far ahead. But maybe that's because it's hard to envision you in a Helga role. Now, a French maid's uniform and a pink feather duster—"

She thwapped him with her magazine.

"Ow!" Richly deserved, he'd admit, but his arm was stinging. "Did you have to do that so hard?"

"Yes," she said, casually returning to the recipe she'd been examining. "That was my version of strict."

"Hmm." And yet, he found her sense of pride sexy. There was no surrender in Cissy. Not on the man-woman thing. Some women would give up anything, even their pride, to catch a man. Not her. But, in other ways, *surrender* was such a desirable word. There was sexual surrender—he'd enjoy that. There was—

"I can feel your panic button pushing," she said, snagging his attention away from surrenders he'd like Cissy to engage in. "You're thinking about it."

"About what?"

"Sex. French maid costumes."

"And the problem with that is…?"

She closed the magazine and picked up another from her big bag. "You want me too much. And you can't have me. Not the way you're thinking, anyway. If Last suspects your marriage is only sexual, he'll know you're not working on the intimacy thing. And he'll never get off your case once we divorce. You'll have accomplished nothing. Remember that. You're going to have to go deeper in your psyche to satisfy him."

His jaw sagged as he realized she'd just escaped through a trap door of her own. She had the whole thing figured out, and it didn't include fantasies of him. "Well, howdy doody," he said.

"It's probably a good thing we're only going to make love once. It'll make you focus on the matter most important to you, which is rebooting your relationship with your brothers. I think I'll take a nap," she said, putting her magazine away and closing her eyes.

He was speechless. No woman had ever said such a thing to him. Cissy had seduced him in a stall and given him her virginity and left her Make My Day panties in the straw. She was gorgeous and he wanted her six ways from Sunday, and they'd tied their marriage to *Once*. One hand in the bag of potato chips. One football game on Sunday.

Only this was far, far worse. He glanced at her in the seat next to him, all long and silver and womanly, and his jeans got so tight he thought he might explode.

He had so many sexual fantasies about her that

once was never going to cut it. But all she'd asked for was one romantic night under the stars. Romantic! He wanted to keep her in a remote cabin for a year and take her until they both fainted from exhaustion. Feast on the meal he'd only heretofore snacked on.

But once more was enough for her? Jeez. A guy could get a complex! "We're here," he said, back to grouchy. "And *just* in the nick of time."

CISSY STARED AT THE embankment. "What are we doing? Why aren't we going up to his cabin like normal visitors? Hannah said he has a honeymoon cabin up there."

"Because when I phoned ahead to tell Hawk that we were coming, he said to meet him in the cave. Do you know where that is?"

"I do," Cissy said, "but I'd prefer not to go there dressed like this." She indicated her high heels and business-like skirt. Even on the side of a dusty arroyo, she was gorgeous. "You know, the way Ranger got down there was by sudden force. Rolling and cursing, going quickly with the flow of gravity."

"I prefer a more dignified approach."

"Hey," Hawk said, coming into view. "Please do not fall down the way your brother did. I wasn't sure we were going to get all the cactus needles out of him."

Hawk shook Tex's hand and kissed Cissy on the cheek. Then he looked at the two of them speculatively. "So. I like what I see. You two are happy together."

"Well, we're necessary to each other," Cissy said.

"That's right," Tex agreed. "Necessary."

"Okay. Come on." Hawk laughed, leading them along the road and down a shorter path into the arroyo.

The hidden totems and cave were just as breathtaking as she remembered. "It's so pretty," she whispered to Tex. "Your brother found this place. Can you imagine?"

"Rolling down here? No. He's lucky not to be permanently scrambled."

Into the cave they went. "This is where I will perform the ceremony," Hawk said.

"You're wearing jeans," Tex pointed out. "And you're barefoot."

"Were you expecting a headdress?" Hawk asked with a grin. "Your brother wasn't worried about me. He just wanted to be married to Hannah, however it happened."

"Hmm," Tex said, and Cissy looked at him.

"Did you need something more rigid?" she asked. "I can accept unstructured…for what we're doing."

"I guess," Tex said, and Hawk nodded.

"You're a man of the soil and think things should be a certain way," Hawk said. "Very hard to change your mind once it's set."

"Whatever," Tex said. "Let's just do this."

"Do you love her?" Hawk asked.

Tex shook his head. "We're not right for each other."

"But you love her."

Cissy stared at Tex, hanging on to his every word.

"Well, I like her. And she's gorgeous. But we're not forever, you know what I mean? She thinks that, too."

"Do you love him?" Hawk asked.

Cissy hesitated. Of course, she had fallen for Tex the first time they'd made love. She'd left Lonely Hearts Station with Hannah to get away from the memory of him, because something about Tex made her evaluate how lonely she was. How much she wanted her life to change. Hannah was running away, and Cissy had wanted to join her, to start life over on a riverboat.

Nothing had gone according to plan.

"Do you love him, Cissy Kisserton?" Hawk repeated.

But Tex was right. They weren't right for each other. She didn't want another marriage of convenience, with verbal prenups. "I thought I did once," she said softly.

Tex turned to stare at her. "You did?"

"But that was a long time ago," she added. "Now we're partners."

Hawk nodded. "There is only one problem in this union. Neither one of you is honest with yourselves. There's too much pain in your past. You both need time to learn from the pain. However, marriage is a matter of learning together. So this is good. Now I will perform the marriage ceremony."

And before Cissy knew what was happening, she was wearing a rope ring like Hannah had worn. Tex was wearing one, too. And Hawk's arms rose up as he called to the sky. She sneaked a peek at Tex and caught him sneaking a peek at her.

And something between them sparked.

Though they weren't touching, Cissy would have sworn it was static electricity. The surprised look on Tex's face told her that he'd felt it, too.

"Now, rub this dirt across each other's faces," Hawk instructed, "to complete the marriage ritual."

Hesitating only a second—had Hannah and Ranger done this?—Cissy dirtied Tex's face. Efficiently and thoroughly.

And he repaid the action, happily dirtying her face until she realized his hands had slowed as his sweeping motions turned to gentle strokes. Then he was holding her face in one hand.

Hawk disappeared.

The hand holding the dirt emptied so that Tex could hold her face in both hands. And then he kissed her the way she'd never been kissed in her life, gentle and timeless as her heart raced inside her. As if she were a true bride.

"Thank you for marrying me," Tex said. "I'm honored that you will be my wife, even for three months."

"Thank you for rescuing me," she replied. "I'm free now. Really free."

"I'm the one who's really free," Tex said. "And you have no idea how much it's going to change my life. For the good."

He buried his hands in her long hair and pulled her to him, his mouth burning against hers before traveling down her throat.

She wanted to tell him, she had to tell him the truth about her feelings, but the way he was kissing her stole her breath and then her courage failed her.

But Hawk had guessed correctly.

TEX RELUCTANTLY PULLED AWAY from Cissy as Hawk stepped back into the cave.

"Honeymoon?" Hawk asked, and Tex shook his head.

"We don't have time," he said. "We're staying on the move."

"Good plan. The first thing I suggest you do," Hawk said, "is head to the courthouse and take out a marriage license. Then get your blood tests. Three days for legality on blood tests. After we get the go-ahead on those, we do a conventional ceremony that will satisfy those people who might try to claim that a Native American wedding ceremony isn't legit."

Tex nodded. "Good plan."

"Now." Hawk sat down cross-legged in the dirt and motioned for Cissy to sit on a nearby rock. "You said there was something you wanted to ask of me besides a marriage ritual."

Tex took a deep breath. "Hawk, we need to hire you. Cissy's got family that disappeared in South America while on a church mission."

Cissy dug in her purse. "I have money to pay you. It may not cover all of your expenses, but it's a start." Her eyes filled. "You're my only hope. No one seems to have any information on my family."

Hawk looked from one of them to the other, not reaching out to take the money she offered.

"There are nine young children who need their parents to come home," Tex said gravely. "If, God forbid, Cissy's siblings are not alive, then we need to know that for the children's sakes. Growing up not knowing what happened to their parents is too much for this family to bear." His voice turned deep with seriousness. "It's a lot to ask of you. I'll go with you if you feel that it's best. I know you find missing persons. And we need someone who can work from a somewhat cold trail and uncooperative environment."

Hawk nodded. "I understand. Yes, I have experience in tracking in South America, as well as other continents. Missing persons can turn up any place in the world." He looked at Cissy. "It could take time," he warned. "And the end result might not be happy."

She nodded her understanding, and Tex was proud of her calmness. "But as Tex said, we all need to know what's happened to them. It's the not knowing that's the worst."

After a moment, Hawk took the money from Cissy and put the envelope in his pocket.

Tex reached over to take her hand in his.

Hawk drew a circle in the dirt in front of him. He laid tiny pebbles inside it without explanation. "What are your plans now?"

"We're heading to Jellyfish's riverboat. Cissy and I can keep moving there. And she can take the job Jellyfish offered her, which is her preference."

"Good." Hawk rose. "I will ride with you. I

won't be returning here for a while. Jellyfish can accompany me to South America.''

"Why Jellyfish? I'm going," Tex said.

"Stay and protect your wife," Hawk said. "That is what you are meant to do."

Chapter Twelve

The three of them piled into Tex's truck, Cissy in front with her husband and Hawk in the back.

"By the way," Tex said, "what does the dirt on our faces mean?"

"That you need to wash it," Hawk said.

"Okay. But why did we do it? What was the symbolic meaning?"

"There wasn't any. It was meant to bring you together. You weren't touching. You were awkward with each other. Marriage grows from two people trusting enough to let themselves be still in another's hands."

Tex glanced at Cissy. They'd fallen for the ploy, and then some. Kissing Cissy was certainly no hardship—and there'd been that strange spark he'd felt between them. Magical and meant to be. Those were the thoughts that had passed through his mind during the ceremony.

"Hey," Hawk said, "Brother Tex, the road is in front of you."

Tex snapped his gaze from Cissy back to the highway. "Sorry."

But he wasn't. He couldn't believe the woman next to him was actually his wife. It felt almost too good to be true. Why wasn't he more jittery about being married?

"When something is right, it is right," Hawk said from the back seat.

Tex's gaze met Hawk's in the mirror. "Why did you agree to do this trip so quickly?"

"Because I wronged Cissy once before, when I did not know her. This is my opportunity to right that." Hawk leaned his head back and closed his eyes. "And I have every expectation that I will be able to find some answers for her."

Tex patted Cissy's knee, enjoying being able to comfort her.

"However," Hawk continued, "I do feel that it would be best if she cuts and dyes her hair. Just for the sake of caution."

"No!" Never in his dreams would he have thought of cutting her beautiful hair off. "Absolutely not. I'll be with her! There's no need."

"I like to cover all the bases," Hawk said. "If you're going to ask me to assist you, you should hear my words. Perhaps Marvella will not come to find Cissy. But if she does, wouldn't you feel better knowing your wife had those few extra seconds of surprise on her side?"

Tex just didn't want to hear it. Her hair! It was so much a part of her.

"Tex, it's hair," Cissy said. "It's not that big a deal."

"It is to me." He adored many things about her, and certainly that was one of his favorites.

"But it makes sense to err on the side of caution. I think I'd feel safer. But maybe that's because I worked in a salon. Hairstyles change often, but not the person."

They were making sense, but he didn't like it. "I'll think about it," he said, trying to be stoic. "Maybe you're being overcautious."

"You'll like my overcautious side if I find her family," Hawk told him, rummaging through a black duffel at his feet. "You wouldn't have hired me if you hadn't expected results."

True. Tex scraped at his chin, imagining Cissy without that long beautiful hair. "It's your choice, babe," he said.

And that was all he could say without his throat closing tightly.

AT THE RIVERBOAT, Jellyfish and Hawk greeted each other like old friends. Jellyfish was clearly delighted to see Cissy, too, picking her up like a doll and whirling her around. "I have a surprise for you," Jellyfish told her.

Hannah and Ranger met her on deck.

"Hannah!" Cissy exclaimed, running to hug her friend.

"You made it back," Hannah said. "I knew Tex would find a way."

They hugged again. "Thanks for sending him," Cissy said. "I'm Mrs. Jefferson now, too!"

"You are?" Hannah pulled back to look at her friend.

"For three months, anyway," Cissy said with a laugh. "Tex thinks that'll get me out of my contract. Marriage, apparently, is good for something."

"So…it's not forever, then?" Hannah blinked at her, then glanced over to where Tex was talking with Hawk and Jellyfish and Ranger.

"No. I wouldn't want that." Cissy smiled at her friend. "Our lives are so different."

"I know. But it's weird how these Jefferson men grow on a woman."

"Hawk's going to go look for my brother and sisters," Cissy said, her tone becoming serious.

"I know. That's why we're here. Jellyfish called me. He wants to take the riverboat up the river, so that Marvella can't locate you easily. He's going to teach Tex how to run it, so Tex can operate it while he's gone. There won't be any customers, because he's shutting down. It'll be you and Tex," Hannah said with a smile. "How does that sound for a honeymoon?"

"Um—" Cissy wasn't certain about the plans that had been made on her behalf. "I don't know what we'd do together for that long, alone."

Hannah winked at her. "You're with a Jefferson male. Trust me. You'll *love* being alone with him."

Cissy laughed. "Maybe they're not all alike. This one has some very specific hang-ups."

"It's all going to work out."

Hannah's confidence made Cissy feel better. "I

have a favor to ask of you," she said, and with a careful glance toward Tex, she dragged Hannah off to her room.

"I CAN'T DO IT," Hannah said, staring at Cissy. "Tex will kill me."

"I think I'd better take Hawk's advice." Cissy held out the scissors.

Hannah ignored them. "You don't understand. Those aren't even decent scissors!"

"It doesn't matter. They'll do. I bought them at the drugstore when we made a pit stop, along with hair dye, condoms and a fingernail file. The necessities." She smiled reassuringly at Hannah. "You can do it."

"Could you have bought hair color any darker?" Hannah balked, examining the shade. "You're going to look like Cher in her younger days."

"No, I'm going to look like Meg Ryan with Cher's hair color." She held the scissors out again. "Please, Hannah. Hair grows back. Dye wears off. Peace of mind will do me good."

"All right." Hannah took the scissors from her friend. "Did you say this marriage was supposed to have an expiration of three months? After Tex sees what I do to you, he may not hang around that long."

TWO HOURS AFTER THE WOMEN had disappeared, Tex thought he had the workings of the engine room. Fortunately, they'd be parked in a safe and distant location while Jellyfish was gone, and there was always Hannah to call and question. She knew a lot about the boat. Ranger had been listening and learning as well. Tex felt pretty certain he could handle the task ahead of him.

But then a dark-haired hottie walked on deck, and he wondered if she was lost. She was staring at him as if he should recognize her, but he'd never seen her before in his life. He started to ask Hawk, Ranger or Jellyfish if they knew her, and then she smiled. His heart dropped into his boots. "Cissy!"

The look was exotic, and somehow highlighted her fragility. He would never have wanted her hair so short, but the strands saucily touched her earlobes, framing her face. Tousled bangs emphasized her magnificent aquamarine eyes. The look was perfect.

"Dang!" he exclaimed. "I don't think I'm going to be able to quit at Once," he told her. "And I have to admit that I had no idea what I was talking about when I said you shouldn't cut your hair."

The men looked at him strangely, but Cissy laughed, knowing exactly what he meant.

"You're safe now," Tex said huskily, going to touch her hair. "From everyone but me. It's trashy. Very elegantly trashy. I can easily see you in a lingerie catalogue."

Hannah came out on deck, skulking. "Are you going to kill me?" she asked Tex.

"You get to live another day, sister-in-law," he said cheerfully. "Do you have a French maid's costume on this bathtub?"

CISSY LOVED THE FACT that Tex still found her attractive. Maybe it shouldn't have mattered so much, but his reaction had pleased her. Didn't every woman want to know that the man she liked fancied her no matter how good or how bad she looked?

And the fire that had lit in his eyes had made her feel so good. For a woman whose husband had never noticed her, except at his cocktail parties, she'd loved changing her look and finding that Tex still admired her.

He was very, very sexy, she decided. She liked him watching her the way he was now, when he was supposed to be paying attention to Jellyfish's instructions.

She wasn't certain she could quit at Once, either. For a moment, she considered whether or not they could live together forever, and came up with a vote of no. Then she wondered whether they could have sex for three months in lieu of the sparse marriage they'd agreed on. But that might not be enough.

She was stuck somewhere between three months and forever.

The men walked over to join the women. Jellyfish wrapped Cissy in a giant bear hug. "Now, listen, because this is important," he told her. "Brother Hawk and I are going to do our darnedest to find out something about your family. Do not worry about this. And most especially, do not worry about this boat, should Brother Tex screw up."

The menfolk all guffawed at that.

"We understand he may have other things on his mind," Jellyfish continued. "The truth is, I'm going to be selling this riverboat, so it'd be no loss if he floats it out to the Gulf or something. If you need to abandon ship, do so. Safety first, my friend,'' he said to Cissy.

"I really appreciate this,'' she told him. "You have no idea how much.''

"I do. Believe me, I do. Ask Hannah about our childhood in the commune, and how we understand one another. We know all about family ties and other matters that bind. Now, I want you to go get some sleep.''

And that raised an excellent question. Were she and Tex sleeping together?

Since everyone on the boat knew the situation, there was an awkward pause.

"Well,'' Hannah said after a moment, "Cissy can sleep in my room like she did before. Ranger and I can take another cabin.''

"You know,'' Cissy said softly as she glanced at Ranger, "if you don't mind, I think tonight I'll sleep under the stars on one of those lounge chairs.''

"That doesn't sound comfortable at all,'' Hawk pointed out. "I'll take a cabin.''

But Tex grinned at her. "I find lounge chairs quite comfortable,'' he said to Cissy. "Come on. Let's go bunk down.''

THEY PUT TWO LOUNGE CHAIRS together and laid a big blanket over them. Then Tex took his bride in his arms and held her tight as the boat floated quietly upstream. "Hey,'' he said to her. "Are you counting stars?''

She sighed contentedly, and he liked the sound.

"I'm counting stars. I don't think I've ever been so happy, in spite of everything."

"I was thinking that the kids would like this riverboat a lot."

"What kids?"

"Your kids," Tex said. "All nine of them."

She rolled over to face him. "Have you lost your mind?"

"I don't think so. Why?"

"Since when do you think about my nieces and nephews?"

He tried a shrug but he was holding her too close and not about to give an inch. "Since I'm thinking of you," he said simply.

"Please stop," she said softly. "You're making me fall in love with you, and I don't want to."

"Well, I'd tell you to stop, but Brother Hawk said we weren't being honest with ourselves, and so I have to let you do whatever you want to do."

"This is a serious matter. I want us to stay within our original terms. Hearts intact, missions accomplished."

"It sounds good on paper, doesn't it?" He yawned in her ear. "Okay. We'll strive for that. Don't fall in love with me."

She pinched his arm. "Are you falling in love with me?"

"No. I'm too emotionally stunted to fall in love. Remember? I'm the surface guy."

"Whatever. I'll miss you when you're gone."

He yawned again. "Where am I going?"

"Divorce court, dummy?"

"Oh, yeah. That's right. Three months and counting from today. I'll be there. Will you?"

"Of course," she replied, her tone light.

"Reality would wear us down, you know. I've got to get back to work. I can't float on this crick forever."

"No argument here."

"And where would we live? You'd never survive at Malfunction Junction."

"Again, no argument."

"And those little children are probably going to need you more than ever, when Hawk gets back."

"I know."

He heard the sadness in her tone. "I'm sorry I'm not the perfect rescue. If I could be your prince, I would be."

"It's cool," Cissy said, her voice sleepy. "If I could be your princess, I might. But for now, do you think you could hush? I want to listen to the water and the engine and the crickets on the banks."

"Sure. I can be quiet," he said, and then he was, but his mind and body were in an uproar he had never experienced before.

In the morning, Jellyfish showed Tex how to dock the boat. Last questions were asked, and then Jellyfish and Hawk said goodbye.

"Do you want us to stay another day?" Hannah asked, clearly worried as she saw the tears gathering in Cissy's eyes.

"No. You've got all that driving to do. But thanks."

Hannah hugged her. "All right. Call us if you need anything, because driving's all we do on our version of a honeymoon. At least for this first year, we're touring, and touring can be interrupted."

"All right." Cissy bit back tears as she waved goodbye to everyone, and then she and Tex were alone.

And then the tears flowed.

"It's all right," he said. "Let's go fishing. Skinny-dipping. Something."

"You're very brave to be trapped on the water with a worried female."

"It's a hardship, but I can manage." Tex dragged her over to the side. "And anyway, I have a little surprise for you."

Chapter Thirteen

"Surprise?" Cissy asked. "Last time you surprised me, I think you jumped out my window."

"I'm not jumping anywhere this time." He tapped her lightly on the nose. "And you'll see soon enough."

They heard footsteps on the boat, heavy feet. "That must be Ranger," she said, turning, only to hear the sound of male voices.

Tex waved her downstairs. Quietly, she faded into a corridor, waiting under the stairwell in case Tex needed her help. She couldn't do much, but she wasn't going to leave him.

"Well, hello, Officers," she heard Tex say. "If you're coming aboard for lunch, I'm afraid the boat is closed for a week or two."

"We're looking for a female by the name of Cissy Kisserton."

Cissy gasped, then covered her mouth.

"Have you seen her?"

"What would you want with her?" Tex asked.

"We need to turn her over to the authorities in

Dallas. Apparently, she's accused of theft by her employer. Have you seen her, sir?''

"She's my wife," Tex said, and Cissy closed her eyes.

"Hmm. This paperwork doesn't say anything about a husband. Single female, white, blond hair, blue eyes—''

"That's Cissy," Tex said, "but she wouldn't steal anything. What's she accused of taking?''

"We can't answer those questions. She needs to come with us, so that we can give her over to the proper authorities in Texas. They can tell you anything you need to know.''

"But she's been with me," Tex argued. "How could she have stolen something?''

Cissy clasped her hands together. She could go out the back door and escape, but that would put her on the run. She was tired of running. She could stay and face whatever charges Marvella had brought against her—which wouldn't stand up in court.

On the other hand, it could take a long time to resolve.

"When were you married?" an officer asked Tex.

"Yesterday."

"But this says Miss Kisserton left her employer's house yesterday. How could you have gotten married? Had the marriage license been applied for previously?''

"We don't have a marriage license. We were married by a medicine man.''

The officers laughed.

"I'm afraid you'll have to turn her over to us. We're sorry."

After a moment, Tex called down to her. "Cissy?"

Slowly, she went up the stairs.

The officers stared at her.

"You're not a blond female," one pointed out. "You have very short, extremely dark hair." He glared at Tex as if there was a joke being played on him.

"Are you Cissy Kisserton?" the other officer asked.

"Yes," she said softly.

"Hey, Marvella," he called. "She's here." And they began stripping off their officer's uniforms. "Dang, that's hot," he said. "How do those cops wear those stupid things?"

Cissy clutched Tex's hand as Marvella came into view.

"They're not married," one of the fake cops said. "Unless you count a voodoo license."

But Marvella wasn't listening. Disbelieving, she approached Cissy, touching her hair with one finger. "Your hair," she said. "Your beautiful hair. What have you done?"

And then Cissy remembered the Ugly Clause in the contract that Mimi had mentioned. "I cut it off. It's gone forever."

"Sexy, isn't it?" Tex said cheerfully. "She's got that trashy kind of thing going now, doesn't she?"

Marvella rubbed a strand of Cissy's hair between two fingers. "Tell me this is dye that washes off."

"Permanent," Cissy said. "Blondes do not have more fun."

"You've ruined yourself," Marvella said. "Who do you think will ever want you like this? It would take two years for your hair to get that long again. Maybe three!"

"And that's past the term of the contract," Tex said cheerfully.

"You're damaged goods," Marvella stated, suddenly wrathful. "All that elegance down the drain. This is all your fault!" she said to Tex.

"Actually, I'm the innocent party here. I didn't want her to change anything, either. But it's what she wanted, and you know, I like her doing what she wants."

But Marvella could only shake her head. "You're worth nothing to me now."

Cissy touched the strands of hair at her neck, staring at her employer.

"If she's worth nothing to you, how 'bout you leave, then?" Tex suggested. "And take your goons with you. Because we've got some serious plans."

"How about I have my goons take care of your smart mouth?" Marvella snapped. "Out here, no one would know what happened to you. And then I could let them have Cissy for all their hard work."

Fear ran through Cissy, until the sounds of truck doors slamming and kids running toward the boat, yelling "Aunt Cissy! Aunt Cissy!" caught her attention.

Four Jefferson men ran toward the boat to keep up

with the kids. "How-dee!" Navarro called. "Boy, is this some setup or what?"

Last skidded to a halt when he saw Marvella and her goons. "What's going on here?" he demanded.

When they didn't reply, he put his fingers in his teeth and whistled sharply. "Boys! We got ourselves some trouble!"

Instantly, the Jefferson men jumped onto the boat, heading with whoops toward Marvella's hired guns. Cissy shooed the children downstairs so they wouldn't get caught in the melee. She heard a splash and a shriek as they were heading down the stairs.

"What was that?" the children asked.

The shriek was definitely feminine. "I think the wicked witch just took a much-needed bath," she told them. "Come on. Let's fix you some peanut-butter-and-jelly sandwiches."

"Are they fighting?" one of the children asked.

"No," Cissy said with a smile. "The Jefferson brothers are just having a little fun."

"I want to go have some fun!"

"Not that kind of fun. You sit right here and I'll fix you some grape soda." And then Cissy realized that the children were her surprise from Tex, and her heart went finally, irrevocably over the edge.

AFTER THEY'D CALLED the police to take away Marvella and her thugs, the brothers joined Cissy and the children downstairs.

"This reminds me of the old days," Last said cheerfully as he sat at the table with eight of Cissy's nieces and nephews. The baby had stayed home with

Gran. "Only now I'm the biggest at the table," he told the children. "But if you'll notice those ugly knots standing around the room," Last said, pointing to his brothers, "I'm the baby around them."

The children couldn't imagine Last being a "baby" because he was so tall, as all the Jefferson men were. Cissy smiled at their innocent awe. "It's a wonderful surprise," she whispered to Tex. "What made you do it?"

"We might as well kick off our honeymoon with eight little firecrackers," he said. "Besides, I thought Gran would like me better if I gave her a little time-out. She needed a caretaker's respite." He kissed her on the temple. "I love your hair," he said. "Next week, we're going red."

She leaned against him, remembering her part as Last glanced over at them. "You're so adventurous."

"You have no idea. I always considered myself a man of the soil, but now I'm thinking I may go over to the watery side of life."

"You could raise water lilies," Cissy said. "Or cattails."

"Say. Aren't you the bright, helpful one." He tugged gently at her hair.

"So. You really got married," Last said. His brothers looked up at the change of conversation. "I don't know that I believe it."

"Believe it," Tex said. "I hooked this little gal fair and square."

Last frowned. "When did this all come about? I gotta tell you, Mason about jumped through the roof when I told him. He said he's tired of this family running off half cocked, getting married like thieves in the night.''

"Do thieves get married in the night?" Tex asked easily, opening a soda. "I'm thinking they're busy working then."

"You know what I mean," Last said with determination. "You're the fourth brother to just up and marry like it's no big thing. I mean, is it or not?"

"So who's upset? You or Mason?"

"We all are. How would you feel if I got married and didn't tell you?"

Tex thought about that. "Well, it would surprise me, since you've always been the moral compass of the family. But if it was the right thing for you to do, I'd send you a gift and my congratulations."

"Shoot." Last looked at Cissy. "I smell a rat, and his name is Tex."

"No need for you to be so suspicious," she said, smiling sweetly. "Would he have asked you to bring eight kids out here if he didn't have honorable intentions?"

Last rubbed the back of his neck. "You're too good for him," he told Cissy. "If he decides to fade out on you, you can call me."

She sensed he was talking that way just to get a reaction out of Tex. But Tex just shrugged. "Ever the worrier. Eat your jelly sandwich, Last. These little children are monkey-see, monkey-do, and you're the biggest monkey they've seen lately."

BANDERA, CROCKETT, NAVARRO, Last and Tex sat on the lounge chairs or stood at the rail while Cissy put the children down for a nap. The kids had run all over the docks and the surrounding land, throwing pine cones, counting clouds and generally wearing the Jefferson brothers out. Tex grinned, thinking his brothers deserved the workout they'd gotten.

"Hey," he said. "Thanks for bringing the kids. You shoulda seen Cissy's face light up."

"She likes those little barn swallows," Bandera said. "You'd best be careful or you're going to end up pushing a stroller."

"Nah." Tex tossed some peanut shells into the water, watching small fish inspect them curiously.

"We noticed your face lit up pretty good, too, when you realized the cavalry had arrived," Navarro said. "Lucky we weren't letting Last drive or we might have gotten here five minutes after you were taking a dunking."

"True." Tex grinned. "I did think there for a minute that I might have let Cissy down."

Last opened a soda and looked his way. "So is that the trade-off? You take care of Cissy, and get her out of her contract, and she gives you respectability?"

"No!" Tex glared at his brother. "Why can't you believe that our marriage is the real deal?"

"Because I know you. And by the way, guess who got stuck cleaning up the mess you made in the rose garden? Huh? And I do mean stuck," Last said sourly. "Those thorns were everywhere! Of course, I am always the one who gets to tidy up after you numbskulls."

"Whew," Crockett said. "With Mason as the oldest, and Last as the youngest, we're bookkended by the two family sourpusses.''

Tex grinned. ''You know, it's not as bad having a few of us around. It's the total sum that's irritating.''

''Yeah, but I miss Frisco Joe, and Ranger, and Laredo,'' Bandera said.

Tex tossed a peanut shell and thought about Laredo. ''I thought I'd miss my twin, but it's not as hard as I thought, since I know he's happy.''

''Yeah, but everybody moved away. Even you're moving away,'' Last said.

''No. I'm not.'' Tex shook his head.

Nobody said anything and he glanced up, seeing all his brothers staring at him.

''Do you mean that Cissy's coming to live at the ranch?'' Last asked. ''There'll be a woman there besides Helga?''

Navarro, Crockett and Bandera began clapping. ''No, no, that's not what I meant,'' Tex said, his face turning red. ''Of course I wouldn't bring Cissy to live at Malfunction Junction. That'd be the worst thing that could happen to her.''

''Dang,'' Navarro said. ''It wouldn't hurt for our female population to grow. Cissy might have some friends who could liven things up a bit.''

''Or, most important, take Mason off our hands,'' Crockett said, to which Navarro and Bandera huzzahed enthusiastically.

Refusing to be sidetracked, Last pinned an eagle's eye on Tex. ''So,'' Last said, ''help me out here with the logistics. How's Cissy not going to live at Malfunction Junction, but you're not moving away?''

WHEN THE CHILDREN AWAKENED from their nap, Cissy led them upstairs to have a snack. The brothers took them swimming, and when the children tired of riding around on the men's backs, they went on deck and opened a can of corn to toss to the fish.

It was the most fun Cissy could remember having.

Last sidled up to her while she was laying little shirts over a rail to dry. ''I hope you'll call us if you need anything now that you're part of the family.''

She smiled at him. ''Tex and I will be fine. But thank you.''

''You make sure he treats you right,'' Last said eagerly. ''He did marry you legally, didn't he?''

''Yes,'' Cissy said with a laugh. ''Better than legal. He followed in Ranger's footsteps, and I'd say that worked out very well for him and Hannah.''

''Well.'' Last scratched at his neck. ''I guess if two people can stand traveling the country in a truck with nothing but the sound of each other to keep them company besides the radio, then they belong together.''

''You see?'' Cissy turned over a little shirt that was nearly dry. ''Conventional ways are not the only ways.''

''Yeah, but I'd still feel better if he married you in a church,'' Last said hopefully. ''I don't trust Tex. Not to be indelicate, but I know that there was a matter of a contract—''

''And all that is resolved,'' Cissy interrupted.

"The contract was broken by my employer. And Tex hasn't bolted. He doesn't need to stay with me anymore. But he is." She smiled at Last, keeping up her part of the bargain with Tex.

"I guess so." But he didn't look convinced. "Where are you two going to live?"

"I don't know. It's been a whirlwind courtship, hasn't it?"

"That it has." Last stared at her. "Almost too cyclonic."

"Do you have a girlfriend?" she asked.

"Me? No way. I'm too busy taking care of the family to have a girl. Mason thinks he does all the worrying about the Family Problem—that's what he calls it. However, it is actually me who worries with efficacy. I find the solutions."

"Are you glad Tex married me?"

He nodded. "I am. I'm just not certain you didn't get the short end of the stick."

Cissy patted his arm. "I'm the happiest I've been in a long time. And see those children out there sticking Tex up with corn juice? They're getting something they haven't had in a long time."

"Hey, I'm sorry about your family." Last watched the kids chucking corn and laughing when it hit the water. "I worry so much about mine I forget that yours has got a real problem."

"Luckily for me, Tex thought of a way to get some help to look for my siblings. And I know you probably didn't want to come all the way out here today, but I do appreciate you bringing the children. It was generous of Tex to think of it. Actually, Tex has done a lot for me,'' she said, her tone wistful. ''And he's been so undercover and subtle about it that I never realized how much he'd done until now.''

She glanced up, and Last was staring at her with a questioning expression.

''I think it's time for us to take the children back to Gran,'' he said suddenly. ''Cissy, welcome to the family.''

She was fine until he said that. Until then, she hadn't felt guilty about what she was doing.

However, now that she'd spent time with the Jefferson brothers, she realized just how much they needed to believe that they were going to find their own happy endings.

And of course, her relationship with Tex was just a preplanned breakup.

''NOW ARE YOU SATISFIED, little brother?'' the Jefferson brothers asked Last after they'd dropped the children off at Gran's and said goodbye. ''Are you convinced that Tex is over his fear of intimacy?''

''They seem to like each other real well,'' Navarro said.

''They seem to be willing to compromise. Real important in a marriage,'' Crockett added.

''She seems sweet and giving,'' Bandera stated, ''which I thought was a change of pace for Tex since he's always liked fast women.''

Last slapped his knee. ''That's what's bugging me! When I was talking to Cissy about Tex, it was like the light of heaven was shining on her face.

She's falling in love, or is already in love with our ape of a brother. But I'll bet you a month's worth of chores that Tex has already planned his escape route." He glared at them knowingly. "Trust me, this marriage doesn't have the glow of forever on it. And one pretty little lady's going to end up with a very broken heart."

"Oh, for crying out loud, Last!" Crockett exclaimed. "Why do you always have to be the font of knowledge?"

Navarro sighed. "He's annoying, but he's usually freaking *right*."

Chapter Fourteen

The silence that settled over the riverboat that evening was unsettling to Tex. He hadn't realized how much he enjoyed the noise and drama of his brothers and Cissy's kids.

"That was quite a surprise," Cissy told him. "Thank you."

"My version of a wedding gift, under the circumstances," he said, forcing himself to sound casual.

"It was very sweet, particularly as I got you nothing."

He grinned. "I wouldn't say that. I heard you fending Last off quite well."

"I'm not certain he believed me."

"You bought me some credibility, though. And for that, I thank you."

"What are you going to tell your brothers when we get a divorce?"

He shook his head. "That it didn't work out."

"Speaking of not working out, now that Marvella has decided I'm no longer worth her employment, I feel pretty safe skipping the blood test and the legal wedding Hawk suggested."

That caught him by surprise, and maybe even disappointed him a little. "If that's what you want."

"It keeps things from getting sticky. We take off our rope rings, and we go our separate ways."

She was awfully nonchalant for a woman discussing a wedding. Shouldn't she be pressing him to commit further? Cissy was working toward uncommitting him. "Okay."

"Again, thank you, Tex. I really enjoyed seeing my family."

He nodded. "You're welcome."

"And for getting Marvella off my case for good. I feel like a weight has been lifted off me. It's been a long time since I felt like my life might actually start moving forward."

He nodded, not saying that he felt the same. There for a moment, when he realized it was just him and Cissy against two determined hoodlums and one mean woman, he'd been very worried. He'd never been so glad to see his brothers in his life. The cavalry arriving to band together once again.

He was feeling sentimental for the old days, but he wanted to move forward with his life, too. That's why he was here on this riverboat with Cissy.

They looked at each other for a few moments.

"I like your hair better this way. Short and dark is real sexy."

"You like it better?"

Her surprised tone didn't faze him. "It looks more real to me. More you. I guess the darkness brings out your face more, so I'm looking at you instead of your hair. I never realized that's what I was doing before." It bothered him that he was starting to learn more and more things about her.

She blinked. "I think I'll go to bed now."

It was their honeymoon, and yet they were both awkward. "Should I kiss you good-night?"

"No," she said nonchalantly. "You don't have to."

And then she went down the stairs.

Have to? He liked kissing Cissy. He'd loved sleeping with her.

So why was he still up here and she was down there?

Because Last's moral compass had changed direction, pointing to an error in Tex's plan.

"HEY, DAD," MIMI SAID, going to stand at his bedside. "How are you feeling?"

"Better," the sheriff replied. "I'm going to make it another day."

She smiled, holding his hand. "You're going to make it a lot longer than that. The doctor thinks you can go home tomorrow."

"I'll like that." He gazed at her, his eyes more tired than they'd been in his stronger days. "I'm sorry you had to come back early from your honeymoon, Mimi. I really like Brian."

"I know." She stroked his hair away from his face. "Dad, we need to tell folks you're not feeling your best."

After a moment, he slowly nodded. "I know."

"I suggest we ask for a leave of absence. The deputy can head the department until you're back on your feet. That way you don't have to resign your office.''

"True. But once people hear I'm under the weather, they'll start coming to visit. Once they see me, Mimi, they're going to know that this isn't simply a cold.''

Patting his hand, she said, "Dad, would it be so bad to retire? Work a little less?''

"To me, yes. Law enforcement's what I do. Union Junction's been good to me, and I do my best to keep it a safe place for folks to raise their young families. Grow old.'' Sighing, he said, "I planned on going to my grave wearing my star.''

Tears welled in Mimi's eyes. "Well, you're *not* going to your grave. So let's not have any of that talk.'' She took a deep breath. "Dad, I'm expecting a baby. You're going to have a grandchild.''

His eyes widened. "A grandchild?''

She nodded, forcing herself to smile and make the tears go away. "Yes. Someone else in the house besides you and me.''

He grinned. "Well, whaddya know about that? I'm going to be a grandfather! That's something I never thought I'd say, Mimi. A grandbaby! In nine months?'' he asked. "Or maybe less?''

She wished she could speed up the process for him. "Nine months, Daddy. We'll just have to be patient.''

Delight spread over his face. "I can be patient, if it means getting to hold my first grandchild.'' And then he held out his hands for her to come close and hug him. She did, and he whispered "I love you" in her hair.

She closed her eyes against the tears. "I love you, too, Daddy."

"HOW'S THE RUNAWAY MARRIED couple?" Mason demanded as Last and the brothers strode into the room, tossing hats as they entered.

"Running away," Last said. "Maybe *floating* away would be the more operative verb."

"What about Cissy? Is she good enough for him?" Mason demanded. "Or did she rope him in to get out of that damn contract?"

The brothers grunted and threw themselves into various chairs, except Navarro, who went into the kitchen, grabbed a bunch of beer cans, sailing them one by one toward his brothers, who skillfully caught them. "Like seals catching fish tossed by a trainer," he commented.

"Practice makes perfect," Bandera said happily, opening his beer.

"I wish you wouldn't do that," Mason said to Navarro. "Do you realize someone's going to be killed by a flying beer can eventually?"

"My aim's good," Navarro said, coming to join his family in front of the tube.

"Yeah, well, once we have the pitter-patter of little feet around here, there'll be no more lager missiles." Mason looked at Last. "So you got anything else to say on the bride and groom?"

"Yeah. They're the biggest bunch of fakers I ever saw."

Bandera snorted. "Last is always working on a conspiracy theory."

"Hey. I know an imposter marriage when I see it." He shrugged. "It's no different than Mimi's marriage. What I'm seeing is that there's trade-offs in life. People cut deals. Maybe they don't say it up front, but it's implied. And maybe that's why people divorce, when one or both of them step outside the box of implied agreement."

"Jeez," Crockett said with a scowl. "If you'd ever stop sitting on your head for a moment, you might actually start speaking like a human being instead of blah, blah, blah."

"I am a student of human nature," Last told him. "Just because you don't like it and have no talent at studying the same, does not devalue my instincts."

"Criminey." Bandera thumped down his beer. "Somebody please puncture his brain so some of the hot air can escape!"

"Back to the part about Mimi," Mason said slowly. "What did you mean by that?"

"First let me finish what I was saying about Cissy Kisserton Jefferson," Last said airily.

The brothers groaned, realizing they were going to have to sit through Last's postulations.

"That gal is a one-man woman."

Every man in the room focused their attention on Last.

"There's no such thing," Bandera said. "Not when she looks like that. Dang, if she hadn't married Brother Budus, I might have had to ask her out. She made my heart thunder in my chest!"

''Yeah, but any dunce could tell they were in cahoots. Their stories were so crooked a child could figure it out,'' Last said.

''That's true,'' Crockett agreed. ''There were holes.''

Navarro snapped his fingers. ''Maybe she's pregnant and he had to marry her! Remember when there was some discussion between Laredo and Ranger— I think—about Tex eating from the garden of good and evil in the barn in Lonely Hearts Station? That was two months ago, long enough for Cissy to know if something's missing, so to speak.''

''Back to Mimi!'' Mason exclaimed, pounding the table with his fist.

They all stared at him.

''Well, Mason, it's so obvious,'' Last said. ''I like Brian and all, and I know he's busy, but even legal beagles spend time with their new wives.''

''The sheriff's been sick.'' Mason shook his head. ''Mimi spends all her time with her father.''

Last shrugged. ''Just saying. You don't have to listen, you know. And it all happened real quick, right? So…I don't think she's ever gotten over you.''

Mason couldn't help the pleasure that glowed inside him—but then he stamped it out ruthlessly. ''I'm going out.''

The brothers looked at one another after their brother slammed the front door. ''Whoa,'' Crockett said. ''What the hell was that all about?''

''Mimi,'' Navarro stated. ''What's it always been about?''

''He took his keys,'' Bandera said.

"It doesn't matter." Last examined his boots as he glanced around for Helga before putting his feet on the coffee table. "Here's what does matter. I'm going to turn the soil in the bed out back and plant wildflowers."

Crockett frowned. "In Tex's rose bed?"

"Yup."

"You can't." Bandera frowned, too. "That's hallowed ground. It's practically sacred to Tex. He'd feel...desecrated. Violated. Encroached upon."

Last pointed his finger at his brothers. "I don't care how he'd feel. I'm sick of looking at that dead garden. Tex is married now. He can tend his wife, and I will tend his no-rose zone."

Crockett looked at him. "Last, it's a bad idea, I'm pretty sure. That's Tex's space. It's like his shrine to Mom. Even if nothing grows right for him, it's *his* eyesore."

"I don't want to avert my eyes anymore when I'm out back. I'd like to, just once, have a garden party and not be embarrassed by the lack of fruition."

"A garden party?" Navarro laughed. "When was the last time we had any kind of party?"

"When Frisco Joe's wife Annabelle and the baby and all the Lonely Hearts women were here," Last said wistfully. "I sure did enjoy all those girls around. Since then, four brothers have left, and we've got nothing to show for it. No babies. No wives to invite girlfriends over. You know, start up some coffee-klatching. I'd like to hear the sound of womanly laughter."

"Helga doesn't laugh, I'll grant you that," Crockett said. "She drinks lemon juice when she wakes up in the morning."

"It's Mason that lives on the stuff. I'm taking over the garden," Last said with determination. "Something's going to bloom around here if it's the only thing I accomplish this year outside of taking care of the ranch. And then when the garden blooms, I'm inviting the new salon girls out, and we're going to…we're going to have a party."

"Wet T-shirt contest?" Crockett asked hopefully. "Thong archery?"

"*No,*" Last said. "We're going to have every single girl in the county over, and we're going to have our own cowgirl raffle. The Great Cinderella Quest. It worked for Tex. Maybe it'll work for Mason."

"Mason!" the brothers echoed with dismay.

"Yes, Mason," Last said. "If I have to, I'll hire a landscape architect to speed things along!"

TEX WANDERED THE DECKS of the riverboat, making certain everything was secure. He tried not to think about Cissy, which was impossible, and forced his mind to other topics.

But Cissy was downstairs sleeping, and he couldn't help wondering what she was sleeping in. It was, after all, their honeymoon. But he really couldn't call it that, since there was no longer any reason for them to stay together except for loyalty on her part. Her dilemma with Marvella was solved. Being married wasn't required to wait out her family's hopeful return. After his brothers had brought Cissy's kids today, and then willingly jumped into the fray with Marvella's thugs, he'd learned an important lesson: the Jefferson brothers were always going to be there for one another. Sure, they weren't likely to give him a pass any time soon about his so-called intimacy issue, but the teasing wasn't going to kill him.

That left Cissy's request for one night of love-making under the stars still unsatisfied, but it was quite possible she'd changed her mind. Women did change their minds often.

He checked a lock and moved to look at the water, which was calm around the boat. It was a windless night, and the moon shone bright and full and teasingly romantic.

He'd always avoided love by keeping his relationships minimal. That wasn't going to work now, because Cissy was way past minimal with him. Maybe he was hoping she'd changed her mind so that he wouldn't have to make love with her.

Once he allowed that notion to creep into his mind, Tex forced himself to examine why a man wouldn't want to make love to Cissy Kisserton.

He'd taken her virginity. That knowledge was stirring up feelings of possession and male pride inside him that he didn't want to recognize. He did not want to fall in love.

He wasn't going to keep up his end of the bargain. "I just won't do it. I can renege since I didn't know that she was a virgin in the first place. I don't want to be a cad by compounding the error. If a man wants to stay out of trouble, he stays *away* from trouble."

Of course, that's what his brothers had said right

before they'd fallen head over heels. Tex groaned. He was already too close for comfort, he knew, because he couldn't stop thinking about Cissy. He wanted to smell Cissy's neck and touch her skin and listen to her laugh.

"I've got it *bad,*" he complained to himself. "Or I'm getting it, and I don't want it!"

That left him with a couple of options.

He could settle down, like Frisco Joe, Laredo and Ranger. Make some babies, go to bed every night with the same woman, enjoy the creature comforts of stability.

Or he could point out the obvious, that she was safe now and no longer needed him, and therefore he was going to be a gentleman and not make good on the lovemaking issue since…since their marriage would be so abbreviated. It was chivalrous to allow her a way out of her request.

Hmm. "The second option has the feel of honor to it," he murmured. Last couldn't say he was being intimacy-stunted if Cissy chose to opt out of the marriage. Drumming his fingers on the rail, Tex decided he would put the question to Cissy at the first opportunity.

It was the gallant thing to do.

"Tex?"

He jumped at the sound of Cissy's voice. "Whew! I didn't hear you come up the stairs."

She patted his arm. "Sorry. I could tell your thoughts were somewhere else."

Yeah, like on you. "Can't sleep?"

"Not really. I'm not sure why."

She laid her head against his shoulder. His heart began beating a frantic tattoo. Cissy felt good to him. Them being together felt right. He thought he felt his scalp break out in hives.

"Come to bed, cowboy," she whispered.

Yikes! "Uh—"

She stroked the skin just above his shirt collar and just below his hair. The skin betrayed him, jumping.

"Cold?" she asked.

Hot, hot, hot was more the description. Tex cleared his throat. "Cissy, I was thinking that your problem is solved. Well, the Marvella problem, anyway. So there's really no need for us to continue our marriage of convenience. I know how you feel about marriages of convenience, so valor and decency compel me to allow you to end our bargain."

"Whatever you say," she said easily. "But valor and decency compel me to point out that I have no panties on under this nightgown."

His throat dried out and that traitorous thing in his jeans zapped poker-straight, the way it always seemed to around Cissy. It was like a freaking homing pigeon, and Tex could only be glad of the cover of darkness, or Cissy would know just what she did to him.

She put her hand against him, finding what he wanted so badly to hide. In that split second, he knew that whatever Cissy wanted, Cissy was going to have.

"Come to bed," she whispered.

He swept her into his arms and carried her down the stairs.

Chapter Fifteen

"I should have sent you home with your nieces and nephews," Tex murmured against Cissy's hair. "I need distance to resist you."

"But then your brothers would have known that we were married for appearances," she pointed out, happy to be in Tex's arms. "And then you would never convince them that you're okay."

"Okay?"

"Yeah. Normal."

"I am normal!"

"Oh, you don't have to convince me," Cissy said. "I've had you. I know you're better than normal. In fact, I don't care whether you're intimacy-stunted or not."

He frowned. "You don't?"

"No. I care about you making love to me again, only this time I want you to stay in the saddle for a *long* time."

He thought maybe his wildest fantasies were coming true—and at the same time, his worst nightmares. "You might be scaring me."

"Will I scare you more if I tell you that when we

stopped at the drugstore for necessities, I also picked up condoms?'' She licked and then kissed his neck meaningfully.

Kicking open the bedroom door, he said, ''I'm encouraged, not scared. I'll be more encouraged if you tell me you bought the jumbo box.''

She laughed. ''I think we'll have plenty.''

He laid her on the bed, watching her move with an eagle eye. ''I've waited a long time for this.''

''You? How about me? I didn't think I'd ever break down your walls. For a while, I was beginning to wonder who the virgin was.''

He ripped off his shirt and lost his boots and jeans somewhere on the floor. ''I'll show you virgin,'' he said with a growl, moving onto the bed beside her. ''What do you mean, break down my walls?''

''I could tell you were battling with your conscience. Right versus wrong. Good versus evil. Take her or not take her. I could tell you were having a herculean struggle with your man issues.''

''Man issues?'' He checked out the color of her toenails and decided he would adore pink for the rest of his life. She had delicate, well-shaped feet and ankles.

''The intimacy thing.''

She ran her fingers through his hair, and he knew nothing had ever felt so good as a woman who knew how to scrape her nails gently along a man's scalp.

''But I knew that in the end, I would have you,'' she said.

''And how do you know I was suffering such a division of need versus deed over you?'' he asked, running a light hand up her arm before taking her hand in his to kiss her fingertips.

"You were wearing out the deck up there," Cissy said with a giggle. "You were right over my room. Stomp! Stomp! Stomp! I gave you time to think about it, and then when I realized you might actually manage mind over matter, I decided to bring you over to the dark side."

He ran a finger along her newly exposed neck. "You did?"

"Yes. It's working, too. Jellyfish isn't going to have to replace the deck, after all."

She giggled again, and that sound alone was enough to give him an instant hard-on. He ran a hand up under her nightgown to give her some of her own medicine and stopped at her hip. "You're *not* wearing any panties."

"Well, I was prepared to toss my nightgown into the water if you didn't agree to get into my bed," she said. "Knowing the hero you are, I was afraid you'd go into the water to save it. I wanted to keep your attention fully on me."

She pulled her nightgown off and dropped it to the floor. He'd never seen Cissy Kisserton naked. The sight was enough to bring a grown man to his knees to praise the forces that had created her.

But it was the sudden question in her eyes that charmed him the most. She looked sweet and vulnerable, and he adored her innocence.

"You have my full, complete, total, undivided attention," he said, almost growling his desire. "And you're going to have it until the sun rises."

WHEN TEX AWAKENED, CISSY was gone. At first that unnerved him, since the night they'd spent together had been so passionate he hadn't considered getting out of bed unless there was a fire. Instantly, he worried that she might have deserted him, now that she had gotten what she wanted. She could have taken his truck keys and ditched him. She could have gone home to her kids.

Hopping out of bed, he reached for his jeans, fumbling around in the pocket until he found his keys, his wallet and his knife. "Whew," he said. Then he heard light footsteps above, and he relaxed. She was probably fixing him breakfast.

But just in case she wasn't, he decided he'd best go check on her. He dressed with lightning, careless speed. It was the first time he'd ever worried about whether or not a woman had enjoyed sex with him, and he really didn't like feeling insecure.

At the same time, they could now call their bargain square. He should be relieved.

And he would be relieved when he laid eyes on her and made sure she was as happy as she'd sounded all night long. "Cissy!" he hollered, hitting the stairs and then the deck in record time. "Hey—"

She turned from her place at the rail and smiled at him like the sun. She was wearing a yellow halter-back sundress with big orange and black flowers. It blew gently around her knees, fluttering delicately with each puff of wind. And she was barefoot.

He gulped, running a hand through his hair and feeling a bit awkward. She looked sexy as anything he'd ever imagined. He wanted to carry her back downstairs! What was the matter with him? She would think he was a Neanderthal if he jumped on her. Now that they were even, maybe she didn't want him anymore. She had specified one night. He took a deep breath and told himself to look only into her eyes. "What are you doing?"

"Feeding the fish." She tossed corn from a bowl into the water. "I plan on feeding you eggs, though."

He went to stand beside her, acting as if he wanted to look down into the water at the fish, too, but all he really wanted was to stand close to her. "You smell good."

"Eggs would smell good."

"Maybe I should shower before breakfast," he said, realizing her hair smelled good and her body smelled good and even the damn corn in her hands smelled good. He developed an instant erection. "I'll be right back."

"What about breakfast?" she called after him.

"I'm not horny!" he yelled back. "I mean, hungry!"

He could not keep getting a stiff one every time he got near her or something bad was going to happen. He'd fall in love. He'd never get any work done. He'd become one of those besotted men that couldn't stop yapping about helping their wives sort threads for needlework. She'd dislike him because he was going beyond the bounds of their original agreement.

"Cold shower," he told himself, jumping into the enclosure and letting the spray hit him.

Five minutes later, he was feeling in control of himself. He went back upstairs and joined her at the rail.

She smiled at him, her big aquamarine eyes crinkling at the corners with happiness. "Hey," she said.

"Hey." Mentally, he checked his crotch. All good.

"Ready for breakfast?"

He smiled back easily. "I'm really not hungry just yet. And I think I should cook for you. Or do cleanup. Whichever you prefer."

She tossed the last of the corn into the water and put the bowl on the rail. Her sundress rose lightly with the breeze, teasing her knees. But he was a foot away from her; a great spot to admire and not conquer.

"I'm not wearing any panties," Cissy said. "Which is what I told you last night, and it seemed to work."

He was staring at her bare back, realizing how close he was to heaven since she obviously wasn't wearing a bra, either. His staff of life had noticed how sweet her curves looked in the dress. "Seemed to work?" he repeated dumbly.

"Maybe it falls under your definition of trashy." She smiled at him. "Or I could undo my halter and see if that works."

The only way he could cool off now was if he jumped overboard and swam a mile. "Cissy—"

She untied the top of her halter and let it drop to her waist. Her breasts were round and beautiful with perfect nipples. All thoughts of staying away from her fled his mind as he pulled her close to him and took a breast in his mouth. She moaned, holding herself up against him, and he swept a hand underneath the skirt to find nothing but a smooth, round bottom.

She was wet between her legs, and he knew the perfect place to cool off.

Turning her toward the rail, he lifted her skirt, holding her tightly against his chest so that he could caress her breasts. Hungrily, he entered her, needing to be inside her and completely aware that he was starting to lose his mind.

And his heart.

TWO HOURS LATER, CISSY awakened from a contented sleep in Tex's arms. After she'd lured him into making love with her again, they'd collapsed on a lawn chair and fallen asleep together.

It was the closest thing to a real marriage she'd ever experienced. "I never want this to end," she murmured.

"I have to say I'm enjoying the benefits of baby-sitting this floating pleasure palace," Tex said.

"It's a nice honeymoon, even if it's fake. I'm going to make you breakfast." She eased off the chair. "I have a new recipe I want you to try. Lie there and don't get a sunburn."

"Sunburn isn't what's going to kill me."

She smiled and hurried down into the kitchen. Twenty minutes later, she returned bearing her creation. "Eggs and sausages and biscuits."

"I'll take it."

She watched with pride as he ate it. "All I get is what Helga cooks, or what we sneak. This is the best breakfast I ever had. Thanks, Cissy."

"You're welcome. But it's a bribe." She winked at him.

"Whatever you want. It's yours. Especially if you're cooking dinner."

"I might. Then again, I might make you do it."

"Hmm." He reached for the orange juice she was holding. "On with the bribe."

"I want to know who tossed Marvella overboard."

"Oh. You want to play twenty questions." He nodded. "I can't tell you. It's confidential."

"Why?"

"Because we Jeffersons never rehearse, review or replay an incident."

"You just let it go."

He nodded happily. "Yes. Once it's over, it's over."

"All right. Why do you stay at the ranch if your brothers make you so nuts?"

A shrug met that question. "They're my family and my job is there."

Same for her, she supposed. "What does Last really want from you? Because I don't exactly see that you have any more intimacy issues than any other man. And trust me, I saw a lot of men come and go through the Never Lonely salon. They all had some kind of issue."

"I guess family members bear down on one another about stupid stuff." He moved the plate to a table and leaned back. "Mason says Last has lollipop-colored vision and he's probably right. Last wants to bring back what we had growing up. But it's not coming back, and the more he pushes, and the more Mason pushes at the family, the more it seems to backfire. Look at me. I could be home doing chores, but I'd rather rescue you."

She smiled. "Only I don't need rescuing anymore."

"Maybe not. But you can't run this big ol' river yacht by yourself."

"It's docked."

"Still, I wouldn't leave you out here in the middle of nowhere."

"You are so gallant." She allowed her gaze to wander over Tex's chest and wondered how she could say what she was about to. "Tex, I'm not going to lure you anymore."

He stared at her. "Why not?"

"It's not right. I have an unfair advantage."

His eyes blinked rapidly. "What?"

"Well, you want sex. I give you sex. It's a bad analogy, but a man's stomach growls when it gets hungry. I feed you. If I didn't feed you, you'd go away."

"No, I'd order pizza." He frowned. "So you're saying that if you don't seduce me, I won't try to get it on my own, and so I'll go away."

"I would have said that if I don't give you sex, you won't ever ask for it, and so it's my fault because I'm playing to your masculine desires."

"Which I'm ignoring."

"I think we covered that last night. I wanted one night of real lovemaking. You were going to think of a noble way out of it. I overcame your resistance."

"Which I appreciate."

"Yes. But if I continue to do that, I'm manipulating you. I don't want that."

He sighed. "Because I'll never seduce you."

"Well, you didn't, even when we were in the barn. If you recall, I came on to you."

He grinned. "Yes, and I appreciated that as well. I would never have had the presence of mind to consider taking you in a barn."

"But if you'd known I was a virgin, you wouldn't have."

"That's right. I…would have…passed."

"You hate admitting that."

"Yes, I do. Because every man probably has fantasized about a virgin at some time or another. I just wasn't ready for mine. But I am now." Reaching over, he pulled her to him, making her straddle him so that she was right over him.

"You're hard again," she said, flattered that he could recover so quickly.

"Yes, and if you're through yakking, you can have me."

He reached under her dress, touching her in places that made her sigh with longing. "I don't want you to think I'm only after you for sex," she said as he undid his jeans. "I am, but I'm not. Does that make sense?"

Pulling a condom from his jeans pocket, he let her help him slide it on. Encircling her waist with his hands, he lifted her, gently positioning her and then sliding her down until he was fully inside her and their bodies were one. "You are after me for sex," he said as she moaned and closed her eyes, "and I'm tossing *all* your panties into the river."

They rocked together slowly until they both reached the point of no return. Almost silently, as if the mood was one of shared serenity, they found fulfillment. Cissy collapsed against Tex and he held her, stroking her back. "I could stay here forever," she murmured. "I love this riverboat."

He gave her a light spanking on her bottom. She gently nipped his earlobe. Last was wrong, Cissy realized. Tex was not afraid of intimacy. She was.

She was afraid that he would know her feelings as well as he was beginning to know her body. Tex was not a complicated man. He lived by a certain set of rules that involved honor and decency. They'd made an agreement. He would honor that agreement.

And when it was over, for him, it would be over.

But she had pride. In her world, there hadn't been happy endings. There were ladies at the salon who received callers who never materialized into permanent relationships, and there was a husband who lied, and siblings and in-laws who disappeared. These moments of pleasure with Tex were her happy ending.

She didn't want him to feel that he couldn't walk away from their short-term marriage. He didn't have to protect her forever. "I can take care of myself," she whispered against his chest.

But he heard her. "Of course you can. That's what I like most about you. You're not the kind of girl a guy has to worry about."

He meant that, of course, to be complimentary. He just didn't realize that she'd fallen in love with her cowboy.

Chapter Sixteen

It was the shrieks of joy that awakened Tex from a sound sleep. He shot to his feet, wondering if the children were back. Swiftly, he checked his jeans and his hair to make sure everything was back in place.

Cissy was going to wear him out—did the woman ever sleep?

Now she was running off the riverboat toward people he didn't know. She flung herself into their arms, and they embraced her. Hawk and Jellyfish were bringing up the rear, and Tex went to meet them.

"How did you manage that?" he asked as he shook hands with Hawk and Jellyfish a safe distance away from the happy reunion. "You can't get to South America and back in two days."

Jellyfish slapped Hawk on the back. "Brother Miracle Worker knows everybody between here and the border. He had this great idea to stop at the military base and ask questions. Request assistance. Grovel for tips."

"I didn't grovel," Hawk said with a grin. But it was clear he was proud of himself.

"So everything in America is locked up tighter

than a drum, right?'' Jellyfish continues. "But not for him. It appears that he has some kind of special—''

"Let's just get on with what happened,'' Hawk interrupted. "No one wants the details. They were on the base, Tex. On the base.''

"Why didn't they call if they were on American soil?''

"Because they were being debriefed. They were getting some medical care and being checked for dehydration and disease, stress, the usual drill. Apparently, they did try to call Cissy, but Marvella told them some sob story about how she'd deserted her and was shacked up with a bad man who threw old ladies into rivers.''

"Oh, yee-haw,'' Tex said.

Jellyfish and Hawk laughed. "At that point,'' Hawk continued, "they decided not to call Gran. They didn't want to worry her since they knew she'd want to call Cissy with the good news. And they sure as hell didn't want Marvella telling Gran what she'd told them.''

"Wise choice. The lady's had her hands full.''

"We figured Cissy and her family would like riding back with you to Union Junction.''

He frowned. "Might as well, since I hadn't planned that far ahead. I certainly had no idea you'd return so soon. But, yeah. I'll take her family back home.'' He didn't say he'd take Cissy anywhere because he wasn't sure where she'd want to go.

"So, I can't accept this money.'' Hawk handed over the cash that Cissy had given to Tex.

"Why don't you give it to Cissy?"

"I have another job lined up," Hawk said, giving Jellyfish a last slap on the back. "And I want to see my arroyo before I go. Keep it cool, Brother Jellyfish, Brother Tex. When next we meet."

He took off walking to the road. Jellyfish and Tex looked at each other. "I'd offer him a ride, but he'd say no."

"That's right," Jellyfish agreed. "Our Native American brother does not ask for favors, and he doesn't say many goodbyes."

"Probably a good thing for everyone to practice sometimes."

"How's my boat?"

Tex grinned. "I love your boat."

"Dude. Buy my boat."

The smile slipped off Tex's face. "What would I do with that caravel of tourism?"

"I don't know. Cissy loves it, though."

"Yeah, well. Riverboats are not part of a cowboy's life. Not permanently. Thanks, though."

"Well, come on. You should meet your in-laws."

"My in-laws!" He looked at Jellyfish, and Jellyfish looked at him strangely. "I mean, my in-laws," Tex amended. "Of course I should meet my in-laws."

But what he noticed was that Cissy hadn't brought her brother and sisters over to meet him. She hadn't even glanced his way. And suddenly, he knew why.

She was going back home. Without him.

"THANK YOU FOR BRINGING ME home, Tex," Cissy said as she walked Tex to his truck four hours later.

It had all happened so fast. She'd said goodbye to Jellyfish and thanked him for letting her hide out there. He'd offered her a job, and she said she'd be back soon, after she reunited her siblings with their children. Cissy wrote a check for the cash that Delilah had given her and mailed it back to Delilah, with grateful thanks for her help.

Tex loaded everyone into his truck, and it was nearly a silent ride to Gran's. Her siblings and their spouses were tired and they slept in the back seat. She read magazines. Tex drove.

The children went ballistic when they saw their weary parents. Cissy had never been so grateful for any sight in her life. She cried, and then she cried again. All she could do was thank God over and over for this precious miracle. And the look in Gran's eyes made everything worth it.

Tex leaned up against his truck, and every once in a while she saw him wipe his eyes. "Thank you," she mouthed to him.

He nodded, and after the children had settled down a bit, she walked over to him. "Are you hungry? Thirsty? Can I offer you anything?"

"I'm going, actually."

She looked into his eyes, seeing what she'd always known would be there. The Great Goodbye. "Is that what you want?"

"You need time with your family. I'd just be underfoot."

"Not underfoot, exactly…"

He put his hand in her hair at the nape of her neck,

caressing her. "Babe, listen. I'm happy I got to see everybody reunited. You can't imagine what witnessing a real family reunion means to me. But you've waited a long time for this, and you need to enjoy it. I don't want to be in the way."

She nodded. "It's not that you'd be in the way, but I understand what you mean."

"We'll see each other again some day."

Her gaze lowered for an instant. "Thanks for everything, Tex. You gave me back my family."

"I'd best head on to mine. Tell everyone I said goodbye."

"All right."

He kissed her palm, waved, got in his truck and drove away.

And it was all she could do not to cry big, fat, slobbery, sentimental tears over the man. But she had a family to put back together, and he had a ranch, and life went on.

ON THE RIDE HOME, Tex thought a lot about what had happened between him and Cissy. On a scale of one to ten, he'd had to give their partnership a ten. They'd made a bargain, they'd kept their bargain, and when they achieved their goals, everybody had walked away happy.

He slipped his rope ring into his jeans pocket. Last was going to bug him to death, but he didn't care any longer what his brother had to say. He and Cissy had the closest thing to a true marriage he'd ever be able to manage.

In fact, it had felt real.

Walking into the house, he found all his brothers sitting at the long plank table in the kitchen eating dinner. They stared at him as if they'd never expected to see him again. And then they glanced at one another.

"Hello to you, too," he said, annoyed.

His brothers mumbled a hello.

"Where's Cissy?" Last asked. "You by yourself?"

"Hawk and Jellyfish brought her family back. They're going to take some time to re-bond," Tex said easily. "I'd be underfoot, and I've got work to do here, anyway. So I figured I'd come back for a while."

"You're not wearing your wedding band," Last observed. "Did you lose it in the river when we were horsing around with the kids?"

"No," Tex said casually. "I'm fixing to go dig up my garden. I've decided to take Mimi's advice and start fresh. Uprooting plants is going to be grimy work and it should take me a couple of weeks to get everything settled. I've got a bunch of plans, and I can't wait to get started." Tex felt good that he had all the answers. There was no need for his brothers to know more than the bare minimum.

"Um, sit down and eat with us," Last said.

"Pass. I've got to do this. It's really on my mind." Leaving the room, he practically flexed his fingers. This was going to be a cleansing. His garden redux. It was time for him to put everything that was unproductive about his life behind him so that he could move forward.

He stopped in his tracks, seeing blooming flowers and small evergreen bushes where his stunted rose-bushes had once struggled. Pink and white begonias, red geraniums. Little signs proclaiming future wild-flowers that would bloom behind these more formal plants. His garden was cultured and planned with fresh plants and compost and even a collection of wire-on-stick dragonflies. Orderly and successful and beautiful. There was a redwood picnic table nearby, with cast-iron tiki torches set into the ground. "Holy cow," he muttered. "I don't believe it."

His solitary Tex-only spot was gone. It was no longer his place.

"Tex," Last said from behind him. "I was going to tell you we made some changes, man. But I didn't expect you home tonight."

Tex stood silently, too angry to speak and too lost to find words.

"I didn't expect you here at *all*," Last told him. "Married guys usually don't return home after a couple of days."

He'd heard it said that every man needed a "cave." This small plot had been that, a place just for him.

Now it had been taken over by his brothers.

"Look, Tex, I get a funny feeling you're more upset about this garden than anything else in your life."

"What's that supposed to mean?"

"I mean, why are you not with your wife? That's bullcrap about her needing time with her family and you having work to do here."

"No, I really do have work to do." Tex held his temper back with difficulty. "And my marriage is none of your business, Last. I know you've appointed yourself the family therapist, but you know what? I don't need any help."

"Gardening might be good for the soul, but it wasn't doing anything for yours. Maybe you should face facts."

"So you helped me by doing this?"

Last looked at him. "I was sick of looking at your scary sticker-land, to be honest. This is inviting. This says the Jefferson brothers aren't totally Malfunction Junction."

All the years that Last had been the baby, Tex and his brothers had looked out for him. They'd protected Last's feelings and covered his ass. But little brother had grown too big for his britches. "Get the hell away from me if this is your idea of an apology."

"I'm not apologizing!"

"I didn't think so. So why are you in my face?"

"I'm just giving you an explanation, bro. I didn't want you stomping all my hard work into the ground just because you couldn't let go."

"Let go?"

"That's right. A man shall leave his home and cleave to his wife," Last paraphrased from the Bible. "Nothing in the book of successful marriage suggests spending honeymoons apart."

"You don't know everything, Last," Tex said, his fury boiling over. Grabbing his brother by the collar, he jerked Last's shirt up over his head so that he couldn't fight. Then he dragged Last over to the newly painted gardening shed and powered him inside. Locking it, he walked away.

Last banged on the door and then opened the side window to yell out, "You can't fool me, Tex! I know an empty garden when I see it!"

Maybe, Tex thought. But that was between him and Cissy.

"DO YOU LOVE HIM?" Gran asked Cissy after they'd helped put the overexcited children to bed. Cissy and Gran had spent the later part of the evening marveling at the miracle that had brought their family back together. After the children went to bed, Cissy and Gran had brought out the fragile painted teapot and the oatmeal raisin cookies, taking them to the wicker table on the enclosed patio. They sat together on the floral-print sofa, enjoying this quiet time together.

"I don't know, Gran. Yes, I love Tex. But I know not to be in love with him. My heart isn't listening to my good sense."

Gran nodded. "He did do a lot for you."

Cissy sipped her tea. "That was the nature of our agreement. There were things each of us needed. When all the requirements were met, the marriage agreement was over."

"And yet couldn't there have been the foundation of a real marriage?"

"I don't hope for that. Tex is the kind of man who treasures his bachelorhood and his lifestyle. He is a nice man. I believe he would always do whatever he could to help me in any way, any time I asked him. But that's not really love," Cissy said. "It's obligation. And chivalry. It's what cowboys do. They work hard. They rescue. They take care of weaker things.''

Gran sighed. ''Do you like this new blackberry tea?''

''I think I do. Where did you buy it?''

''I didn't. Tex brought it to me.''

''He did?''

''Yes. When he slipped me money for the children before he took you to the riverboat.''

Cissy was so surprised she couldn't speak for a moment. ''I had no idea.''

''I imagine not. As you said, cowboys take care of weaker things.''

She shook her head. ''I don't like to be an obligation or a woman a man has to take care of.''

''It does go against the grain,'' Gran agreed. ''Especially for you. You've taken care of us for so long that I believe you've begun to think you can't let anybody take care of you.''

''I feel like you do take care of me, though,'' Cissy protested. ''Having my family back together was all I ever dreamed of.''

''Still, I'd like to see you have something just for you. I wouldn't mind seeing you give your marriage a real chance.''

''I learned a long time ago not to expect more than what I was given.'' Cissy touched Gran's hand. ''Don't worry for me. There was so much more than I ever expected with Tex that I can't be sad. It's over. I truly don't expect to see him again.''

''Will you divorce, then?''

"I suppose. That was always the plan."

"What will you do now?"

Cissy poured herself and Gran more tea. "Jellyfish offered me a job on his boat. He'll be taking a new tour up the river in a week. I can stay here, or I can go on and work. It depends on how much you feel that you need help."

"Truthfully, I feel that the kids will want to spend time with their parents and vice versa. Those kids are going to be in shock for a long time. Good shock, of course, because I know in their hearts they had stopped believing in a miracle."

"I know they had," Cissy said softly. "And it broke my heart."

"You know, your folks would have come back if they could have, Cissy. They didn't mean to leave you kids behind. Drunk drivers are every mother's nightmare—"

"Let's not talk about it," Cissy interrupted. "I think I will go on Jellyfish's new tour. He's got a bunch of international luminaries who called him when he returned from his short jaunt with Hawk. It's part of a tour that wants the full experience of America, and the original boat they'd hired had gotten damaged. So Jellyfish would be happy to have the help, and I'd be happy to have the job."

"And then there's Delilah," Gran reminded her. "She said you could work for her anytime."

"Yes." She looked at her grandmother, her heart wiser than it had been before. "The first time I left Lonely Hearts Station, I was running away from Marvella, and I was running away from Tex. I'd known then I was in danger of falling in love with him. The second time I left Marvella's, he accompanied me, and by then I knew I would need to get away from him if I ever hoped to get over him. All of his brothers frequent Lonely Hearts Station." She sighed. "I want a fresh start."

"You'll enjoy seeing the country, especially by river."

Cissy smiled. "I feel so happy when I'm on the water. I can't even explain how soothing it is."

Gran hugged her tight. "Don't be scared to come back, though. I'll miss you dreadfully. Did I tell you that I love your hair?"

"Do you really?"

"Yes, I do. I loved you blond, but I adore the brunette, too. It's sassy."

"That's what Tex said, too."

"He wasn't afraid of change, then."

Cissy laughed. "Some change, yes."

"But where you were concerned, no."

Cissy sat back, thinking about all the changes Tex had endured to make her happy. "I have a week here, and then I'll take the job hostessing for Jellyfish's month-long excursion. I'll bring you back a souvenir," she told her grandmother to change the subject.

"Just don't bring me a new husband," Gran replied tartly. "I like the one you have."

Chapter Seventeen

For five days, Tex ignored his brothers. He spoke, but in monosyllables, and usually just a grunt as he passed them in the halls.

"It's like he's creating a new language," Last complained as he and Navarro and Crockett watched him out the window. "Sort of like abbreviated verbal sign language in whale pitch."

"Jeez, Last!" Crockett slapped his baby brother upside the head. "What the *hell* did you just say?"

"Lost me," Navarro said. "Look at him out there, all alone, rolling wire by himself like a pariah."

"What I said," Last enunciated, "is that 'uh,' 'ho,' 'yo,' 'hm' doesn't make for successful communication. Instead of moving into the twenty-first century of language skills, Tex is creating an anonymous dialect."

"It's your fault," Crockett told him. "He hasn't wanted anything to do with the family since you tore up his hallowed ground. We told you not to do that!"

"It shouldn't have made this much difference." They watched as Tex clipped some wire and pulled some more. "It's like he's turned into…Mason!" he whispered.

"Do not invoke the *M*-word on Tex," Navarro said. "We wouldn't wish that on a brother."

"Yes, but Last's right. Tex is turning into a solitary bonehead."

"Tex says he's not coming to the party tonight," Last told them. "I told him it was a garden party, and though it was hard to understand in grunt form, I do believe he told me to shove my head up my butt. Or maybe he said 'shut your hat up, Sir Tut,' but I wasn't hanging around long enough to play Professor Higgins."

"It's your fault, dummy." Crockett turned away from the window. "And now you've got all these babes coming here so that you can do this cowgirl raffle thing for Mason, and I'm telling you, you're standing on a landslide. Mason is never going to go so easily into such a trap."

"Maybe that shouldn't be my goal," Last said.

"Have you ever considered that goal planning isn't your thing?" Navarro demanded. "Last, has it ever occurred to you that maybe this isn't the family that's going to see a lot of Hallmark moments?"

"That doesn't mean I should wear a shroud of negativity," Last shot back. "You wear the shroud, and let me shoot for the clouds."

"Whatever." Crockett went into the kitchen. "For a cloud-seeking kind of guy, you sure shot Tex down. And he doesn't have anybody to talk to about it. I mean, he can call his twin, but he won't. And he won't talk to us. So that lonely man you see out there is going to be what he's going to be. Lonely and gardenless."

Navarro thumped Last on the arm as he went to sit across from Crockett. "Usually the family philosopher, this time he's the family Philistine."

"Very funny." Last stared out the window with determination at Tex. "It may be my fault, but that doesn't mean I can't try to apologize. In my own special, optimistic way."

TEX HEADED OVER TO MIMI'S to check out the small pond on the back forty that their properties shared. It was the Cannady pond, though, by the Jefferson's measure, simply because the sheriff had been the one to maintain it over the years. The pond was just right for swimming and even a little paddleboating.

Mimi had suggested he try out his gardener's frustrations on some water lilies, an idea that fairly intrigued him. Rather than put up with the plans for tonight's shindig, he planned to map out his strategy.

There'd be no pressure on him this time, Tex thought with satisfaction. It was Cannady water and a Cannady plan. Failure was an option, which he appreciated. For once, he wanted something that he could create on his own.

And in the back of his mind, he couldn't help some satisfaction that Cissy had playfully suggested water lilies and cattails to him on the river. Maybe it was time to embrace a different plant. And a different mind-set.

"Hey," Mimi said, coming up behind him.

"Hi, Mimi," Tex replied. He pointed around the

plan. "You need a weeping willow out here, too. 'Bout the time the baby's old enough to want to swim, there'll be shade."

"That's a great idea. I've always wanted to landscape this pond. I'm glad you don't mind doing it, because it'll be a job."

He gestured back toward her bounteous rose garden. "Not like you couldn't do it yourself. Your roses are amazing."

"Uh-huh. I'll just watch you turn this pond into what it should be." She sat down cross-legged on the ground, watching him sketch his plans. "Guess you'll be at the garden party tonight."

"Don't think so. Have no desire."

"Why?"

Shaking his head, he said, "Too many reasons to count. I may go into town."

"Or you can stay right here with me after I get home from the hospital. I can feed you dinner, if you don't mind warmed-over lasagna."

"Why don't you want to go to the party?"

"I don't know."

"Yes, you do." Tex gave her a sideways glance. "Mason?"

"Well, maybe. There'll be lots of pretty girls there, and…you know me, Tex."

"Yeah." She'd hired Helga, and no one was ever going to tell him it was for any reason other than to keep Mason safe from female enticement. "How are you feeling?"

"In the mornings, a little strange. Otherwise, fine."

"Sure you don't mind warming up lasagna? I think I'll take you up on the offer. Last has been acting shifty, and I'm afraid he may have something up his sleeve where I'm concerned."

"Like what?"

"Don't know. But when he's got the fix-it bug eating at him, who knows what he'll do. He's even got little name tags on the table at everyone's seat. He called them ice breakers, but I wouldn't count on just ice being broken."

"Oh? Who's seated next to Mason?" Mimi asked too nonchalantly.

Tex shrugged. "I didn't look. I just checked to make certain my name wasn't on the table."

"Well, I'd love to have your company tonight. I'm going to walk over and say hello to the Union Junction Style girls for a minute, but that's all."

She'd beat a hasty retreat if Last put his stupid plan for Mason into action. Tex chose to ignore that he'd participated in a bachelor raffle himself. Last's plan was so dumb it was unbelievable, because Mason would never "win" a woman willingly. "You know, Mimi, I could take you to a movie," he said, knowing how hurt she might be tonight. "Or we could go looking for baby stuff. I would love that."

Her gaze was perceptive. "So, what is it you don't think I should see tonight?"

"Nothing, exactly. As you said, though, it won't be much fun with single girls, single guys, when we're the only married ones. You know. We'd feel like chaperones. I don't want to feel like a chaperone, do you?"

"I also don't want to feel like I'm being baby-sat," Mimi said with spirit. "So why don't you tell me exactly what's happening tonight, or I'm going to be certain that you're baby-sitting me."

Mimi and Cissy were so much alike. He sighed. "I'm not sure, but I know it won't be something I enjoy."

"Are you and Cissy going to stay married? Once you came home, I thought you weren't, but the way you're acting, it sort of feels like you're trying to be faithful and honorable."

"Oh, yeah. That's it," Tex said. "It would be dishonorable to hang around a bunch of single, cute, interesting women."

She stared at him. "Who are you trying to convince? Me or you? Because frankly, I'm starting to think that you really did fall in love with Cissy and just won't let yourself admit it."

He had a sneaky suspicion she was right, but it wouldn't do him any good to let that confession leak. "Let's go shopping for baby clothes. Come on." Helping Mimi to her feet, he practically dragged her to her house.

"But I'm going to the hospital first," Mimi protested. "I want to see Dad. And then I'll swing by and get you, and we'll vacate the premises."

"That's a deal," Tex said with satisfaction. "It'll give me time to shower and keep me out of the range of Last's motives all at the same time!"

TEX HAD BARELY SHOWERED and made it down the stairs before Mason collared him.

"Hey," Mason said. "There's no place card out there for you on the table. Or placard, as Last loves to call them. It's so dopey it's embarrassing. He acts like we're going to be taking high tea with the queen."

"I'm taking Mimi shopping for baby clothes," Tex told his older brother. "As old married folk, Mimi and I feel it incumbent upon ourselves to skip this little shindig."

Mason jerked his head toward the backyard. "Last has me sitting between a brunette and a redhead. There's a blonde sitting across from me, and there are ethnic varieties represented on the diagonals. One might say that I'm surrounded by a smorgasbord of beauty. Which makes me very unhappy."

"Hey, call it a happy accident," Tex said. "I'm outta here."

"Oh, no, you're not." Mason pointed toward the backyard. "You at least have to say hello to our guests for the sake of manners. Especially since our baby romance planner isn't here to do his part as host." Mason's voice dripped with displeasure.

"Where is Last, then?"

"Hell if I know. When he gets here, he's dead, though. He'd better get here," Mason said with determination. "He's been gone for two hours, and if his idea of stirring up romance is to surround me with dolls and then disappear, he's got rocks in his head."

"Yeah, most men would complain about such harsh treatment by their brother." But Tex followed his older brother out to do his duty by the Jefferson name.

"Wow, these girls sure look good for a garden party," Tex said, amazed. "Mason, you should count yourself lucky Last thinks this highly of you. If I were in your shoes, I wouldn't be sharing." He greeted the women who would sit with Mason that night.

"Well, brother, then you must do the honors," Mason said, practically forcing him onto the bench. "And I'll take Mimi shopping for baby clothes."

Tex hopped up off the bench. "Oh, no, I wouldn't think of it. Shopping is so boring. You enjoy these lovely ladies." He gave Mason a shove so that he nearly fell into one of the women's laps.

"Good manners dictates that I, as eldest, make certain that my brothers are all suitably cared for," Mason said between gritted teeth. He got close enough to Tex's ear to mutter, "You have to save me. As you can see, Last has some devious plan for me."

Sighing, Tex sat, forcing a smile for the ladies of Union Junction Style. Once upon a time they'd been Delilah's girls at the Lonely Hearts Salon, and had done a big favor for Union Junction during the big storm. He owed it to them to sit and be a good host.

Mason was right. He could take Mimi shopping for baby clothes, and he, Tex, would not die enjoying the babe lottery seated around him. Sweeping the name tag with Mason's name on it aside, he said, "I'm cutting in on this dance, ladies, if you have no objection."

"No," they all said, smiling. Mason appeared to

give a sigh of relief and began loping toward Mimi's house.

Tex grinned at the ladies around him. Too bad if it messed up Last's plan of finding Mason a woman. One day, Last was going to have to learn not to interfere in people's lives.

"So, it's sure good to see you again," he said gallantly to his guests.

"Hey, everybody," Last said from behind him. "Look who I found."

Tex turned with a preset smile on his face.

Cissy stared at him, and at all the beautiful women next to, across from and on the diagonal to him. Her rivals from the salon days.

"Hi, Cissy," he said weakly, cursing Mason and Last and himself most of all.

"Hi," she replied, taking a visual roll call of his companions.

"I didn't expect you."

"I can tell."

"That's not your place," Last said quickly, trying to do damage control. "Tex, you're not supposed to be here tonight. You said you weren't participating!"

But Cissy had walked to the end of the table and seated herself next to Crockett, so she didn't hear Last's words. Crockett hugged her and acted happy to see her, but Tex wanted to strangle Last. "Last, what are you doing?" he demanded, jumping up to follow his suddenly persnickety brother into the house so their argument wouldn't be broadcasted.

"What are *you* doing?" Last shot back. "That's Mason's seat!"

"He didn't want to sit in it!"

"Well, you shouldn't be. You're married!"

"How could you have brought Cissy here?" Tex demanded, worried that she might think he'd been flirting or worse yet, trying to put the make on other women.

"Excuse me, but she is your wife, I think she has a right to be here. Or maybe she's not your wife, and this whole marriage thing has been bull-malarkey," Last said, his voice ringing with conviction. "You've lied to all of us. You never got married at all!"

It was a comedy of errors, but there wasn't anything funny about it. "I think I'm in big trouble," Tex said. "You're going to have to bail me out."

"I can't. I've got to host this party. As it is, I've wasted two very valuable hours waiting in town for Cissy to get here so that she could follow me to the ranch. Not that I mind. But she got stuck in a traffic jam between here and her home, and got here late, and I've got to get the hors d'oeuvres out. Or maybe we skip the cheese-ball-and-cracker thing and go straight to pouring the ladies wine. You pour, Tex. You don't have anything to do except stand there and frown. It's not my fault you were sitting in the wrong place at the wrong time. I was trying to atone for upsetting you the other night, and thought you'd appreciate getting to see your wife. Obviously, I was so incorrect that I may have hit the *Guinness World Records* book for Incorrectness. If it wasn't a category before, it *is* now."

He was so sanctimonious it was annoying. "I *am* glad to see Cissy. Damn glad to see her! But she's never going to believe that I've thought of only her for the past several days when she's found me surrounded by gorgeous girls." He felt very sorry for himself on this point. How could his life be so upside down? Minutes ago, he and Mimi had been talking about Cissy. Then she appeared in his life and caught him with his hand in the cookie jar. It wasn't fair. "Of course, she could be very mature and forgiving and realize that just because I was seated with women, doesn't necessarily mean anything was going on," Tex said hopefully.

"And pelicans may land in our trees," Last said dolefully. "You've messed up all my plans for the evening. Even Mason's gone. How do all my plans backfire on me?"

"I don't know." Tex gazed out the window at Cissy grimly. "I'm fixing to save mine." Striding out the door, he walked to the table. Cissy looked up at him, but she didn't smile.

"Crockett, change places with me," Tex said.

"No, thanks. This is the best seat in the house."

Cissy smiled at him. Tex began to feel a bit desperate, as if he was the "away" player in a game of "keep away." Navarro was across from Cissy, so Tex tried that next. "Navarro, how about you swap with me?"

"Nope. I'm good." Navarro beamed at him. "Your wife's telling me about the kids. I sure had fun with those little dickens at the river."

Tex thought his brain was beginning to fry between his ears. His brothers were such butts!

"Cissy," he said with determination, "would you like to take a walk with me?"

"I just got out of the car, Tex. I was stuck in traffic, and it was a long drive. I really don't feel like a walk right now." She sipped an iced tea Last put in front of her and turned back to face her seatmates. "Wonderful, Last. You're a wonderful host."

"Fine," Tex said. "I'll just pull up a chair."

He went looking for a chair, but, of course, it was a picnic table with a bench seat so he was making an idle threat. He had three choices, since Cissy was inclined to treat him as if he was just another brother: return to his seat, or go into the house, watch the tube, get out a TV tray and eat in silence.

Or he could go fetch the prince for whom this party was being pitched. That was the best idea. He started toward Mimi's house to tell Mason that he didn't want to relieve him anymore and that he'd just have to return to his seat, but Mimi and Mason were talking on her back porch, swinging in the porch swing. They weren't sitting close, but they were talking. Tex wasn't certain about barging into that particular conversation, so he turned around and headed back. "How was I innocently planning water lilies and cattails and now find myself in the middle of a smackdown?" he groused to himself.

When he got back, Cissy was gone.

"Where'd she go?" he demanded of Crockett and Navarro.

They shrugged. "She said she needed to get back. Lots of stuff to do."

"She just got here!"

"She said the party wasn't what she'd expected," Crockett explained. "I guess Last had convinced her that you wanted to see her, even though you hadn't called her. She said she'd interrupted your good time, and that friends didn't do that to each other."

"I wasn't having a good time," Tex stated. "Did you tell her that?"

"Nah," Navarro replied. "She told Last, nicely of course, that he needed to quit trying to fix you, that you had to fix yourself. Cissy also told us to give you this, and we felt that there was no need to go into deep explanations at that point."

He handed over Cissy's rope ring, and Tex's heart seemed to crash out of his chest. "You know, I can't win. I honestly can't."

"Did you call her since you've been home?" Crockett asked curiously.

"Well…no. But I was going to. I just figured she'd call when she came up for air. I mean, her family just returned. They've got their lives to put back together."

"Bro, you are in a screwy situation. But I think," Navarro said, "that it was her parting words that stalled us."

Crockett looked at him sorrowfully. "She said Last was slightly off the mark. You don't have a reluctance for intimacy per se, just the permanent kind. And that you'd be happy the three months turned out to be more like three weeks, since once you'd played the part of rescuer, you'd forgotten her."

What could he say to that? His behavior branded

him. Maybe all his intentions had been good, but that hadn't been what a marriage required.

"I don't suppose she said whether or not she was returning to Gran's."

"Actually, she did," Crockett said cheerfully. "She was thrilled to be going back to the riverboat. Jellyfish has got a new tour he's working, and she said it was something she was really looking forward to. She'll be gone for a month."

Great. His marriage was over, and his bride was excited about floating away.

Chapter Eighteen

Two weeks later, Cissy felt renewed. Jellyfish treated her like a queen, and she learned to appreciate friends who didn't expect anything but friendship. She learned to be a superlative hostess. Men found her interesting and tried to engage her in more than light conversation. A fast riverboat romance wasn't right for her, even if she could have forgotten the man who'd held her heart.

Mostly, she enjoyed the solitude. After her shifts at night, she sat on deck in a secluded area Jellyfish had roped off with an Employees Only sign and a chair he called his dreaming chair. She didn't dream, but she loved watching the river float past and gazing at the beautiful stars overhead. Every once in a while Jellyfish joined her, but mostly he understood that she needed time to heal.

For the first time in her life, she felt as if she'd found a place of her very own.

TEX LOOKED AT THE ARC of cattails at the top of the pond with satisfaction. "Just look at those beauties," he said to Mimi. "They transplanted better than I would ever have thought. If those live, I'm going to get some more for over there.''

Mimi nodded. ''But I love the weeping willows.''

He'd put five in, spreading them out around the top of the pond. That way the view from the house wasn't blocked. ''Just wait until they're big and full.'' He gave her a mischievous glance. ''Just wait till you are. That's going to be something to see.''

Mimi laughed. ''I'm not showing yet, but then maybe a woman doesn't show quickly her first time.''

''I dunno.'' Tex only knew about cattle. ''Hey, where's Brian these days?''

''Working in Austin. He's got so many high-profile cases right now that he can barely get to the phone to call me.''

Tex frowned. ''Is that hard on you?''

She shook her head. ''Now that Dad's at home, I spend so much time with him that I'd feel guilty if Brian were here. Once Dad is better, I'll be able to be more of a wife. I know Brian loves me. It'll all work out eventually.''

Tex nodded. ''Yeah.'' He hoped so, anyway.

''Marriages don't always have the perfect beginning.''

Pff. Understatement of the year. But he wanted off the subject of marriages. ''So, now I'm thinking we need a boat dock. Not a big one, more like a fishing-pier type of thing.''

''There are no fish.''

''We could stock fish, but I'm not keen on that. If we plan it right and put the pier in the deepest part, the kids could jump off into the water. I know they're going to try to swing from the willow branches, and I'm not particularly sure they'll hold. Pier might be better.''

She gazed up at him. ''Tex? Where are all these kids coming from that you keep talking about? You have three married brothers, and none of them live here. Even so, they have a total between them of one child, Emmie, that I know of. And I'm only having one.''

''Well, I...I don't know,'' he said with wonder. ''I was trying to plan for the future and I kept seeing bunches of kids.''

''But you don't want any.''

''Hell, no, I don't.'' Briefly he thought about Cissy, but she'd also said she didn't want children. ''At least I don't think I do,'' he said slowly. ''There were so many of us that we never got a break from one another. Sometimes we wore one another out.''

She was silent.

''We had you to break up the monotony or we might have killed one another.'' His tone was thoughtful. ''You were like the tribal goddess. We could always count on you to think up a sacrifice.''

She laughed. ''Tex, I wasn't that bad.''

''Yeah, you were. You were fun and interesting, and you and Mason thought up some doozies. We needed the softness of a girl around, even if you were more boy in some ways than girl.''

''Thanks. It was a survival-of-the-fittest thing.''

''I know.'' He scratched his head. ''Hey, why do you think you'll only have one child?''

"I don't know." She shrugged. "I just don't see it. Same way you don't see yourself having any."

"Yeah." He bent down to dig some more dirt out around the weeping willow, not noticing Mimi walk away. The plan called for small circular gardens at the base of each tree, sweet william in each stone-lined circle. It would be dainty and white and—

Slowly, he turned the soil in his hands. It was under his nails and lined his palms. He swept his hands against each other, enjoying the scrubbiness of dirt on his skin. The dirt of his land relaxed him. Like water relaxed Cissy.

They were so different.

Mimi and Brian were married. They had to be apart. It wasn't ideal, but obviously, it had to be that way.

Tex was married to Cissy. She hadn't called, and except for the few moments he'd seen her at the garden party train wreck, they hadn't communicated.

This was a woman who understood that he couldn't pull his head out to save his life. And she was content to walk away, no hard feelings.

He'd spent all this time putting in cattails, not too many, just enough for beautification. And Cissy had mentioned cattails to him. He'd been toying with the idea of floating a water lily or two for a delicate touch of color. She'd teasingly suggested he consider farming water lilies since roses didn't work for him.

Water lilies were plants that survived in water. A plant was a plant, and he loved to garden.

He swept his hands off.

CISSY STOOD AT THE ENTRANCE to the riverboat, greeting the guests returning from a day of shopping and walking in the riverside town of Sperryside. The guests were enjoying the small towns they visited. They liked the privacy Jellyfish's riverboat provided—something they, as famous wealthy people, didn't find very often. The chefs that Jellyfish had hired for the excursion had wowed them. He had four, who rotated weeks of specialties: Louisiana seafood, Mississippi down-home, and more.

"I bought you this," Sheikh Mohammed Fadin said as he returned to the boat. He handed her a beautiful handmade white lace doily. Startled, she glanced at Jellyfish, who stood beside her greeting the returning guests. Imperceptibly, he nodded.

"Thank you," she said to the sheikh. "It's lovely."

"As are you." He nodded slightly and boarded.

Jellyfish grinned at her. "You can't expect not to have an admirer or two."

She looked at him.

"It's okay, Cissy," he said gently. "The sheikh means nothing by it except as a courtesy to his hosts. To refuse it would embarrass him. If he had genuine designs on you, it would have been rubies or something."

She was silent.

"I'm sorry," he said after a moment. "I'm sorry you're so hurt."

She took a deep breath. There was no point in hiding what he obviously knew.

A playwright boarded, handing her a beautiful

stone paperweight mined from local formations. "You shouldn't have," she said with surprise. Jellyfish touched her back, and Cissy said, "It's so pretty. Thank you for thinking of me."

The playwright said, "This has been the trip I needed. Thank you for taking such good care of me. Some of the best hotels in the world haven't done as well. You've got the right touch of warm hospitality and quiet caretaking. I've gotten most of my next play plotted."

She smiled. "I'm so happy. The river probably has more to do with your muse generating, but Jellyfish and I are delighted you're pleased."

The playwright shook Jellyfish's hand and boarded.

"You're such a mother," Jellyfish said with a laugh.

"Mother?"

"Yes. You're mothering the guests like you did your nieces and nephews. The men are eating it up, because every man likes to be attended to, you're beautiful, and they can tell it's sexless. You're the perfect hostess, Cissy."

"I don't know that I want to be sexless," she protested, trying not to laugh. "That sounds sort of scary."

"I didn't say *you* were sexless," he said as they closed the gate behind the last guest. "I said that the way you treated men was sexless. So they can do a little something to thank you and you won't perceive it as flirtation. No, Cissy, there's nothing sexless about you at all. It's just that you're not available, and they can tell.''

''No, I think they're worried that you'll make them walk the plank. You're the largest man any of us have seen.''

''Yeah, I know. The sheikh tried to hire me as a bodyguard.'' Jellyfish laughed. ''But I'm not available, either.''

''I don't understand this 'not available' thing. Could you explain?''

He leaned against the rail, looking out at the sleepy town. ''I'm going to sell my boat, and then…I don't know what. I'm ready to do something else. I grew up in a commune. I want to see the world. This is my pirate phase. I'm going to have another phase soon. That's all I know. So I don't want to be hired or wifed. You're in love, Cissy, and that's why you're not available. Your heart's a little broken, and people can pick up on your sadness.''

''Oh, I'm sorry! I've tried so hard to be cheerful!''

''You have. The guests love you, including the women. It's not obvious, but the sadness shows every once in a while when you look down, like your thoughts are somewhere else. It gives you a very fragile, wistful appeal, and it makes people want to take care of you. Men eat it up, but as you said, any man on board who thought once about flirting with you thought about me next and didn't have a third thought. I am a large pirate, as you noticed.''

She smiled at him. ''Maybe that's why I feel so safe on the riverboat.''

''You just go on figuring out your life, sister

Cissy,'' he said easily. "Don't you worry about a thing. However, if I should see your cowboy one day, do you want me to dunk him or allow him on the boat?''

"Oh, I don't know,'' Cissy said. "He hasn't done anything to be dunked for. So I guess I'd have to say to let him stay dry.''

"You're certain? Because, as captain, I reserve the right to do whatever I want.''

His protectiveness was sweet, but not necessary. "I'm really all right, Jellyfish. But you don't have to worry about Tex anymore. If he was going to talk to me, he's had plenty of time to do it.''

"Okay.'' He looked past her for just an instant, then said, "I'll be starting the boat in five minutes. The guests should be settled by then. You stay here until the boat is moving, and greet any passengers who wish to embark.'' Then he walked away, calling over his shoulder, "And I'll ice extra champagne.''

"Embark?'' She stared after him. They'd counted all their guests. Everyone was aboard. Turning to look into town, she caught her breath.

Tex was jogging toward the boat, his hands full of long-stemmed roses. "Tex!''

"Don't leave without me!'' he called.

She put her hands out to help him from the dock onto the boat, but he vaulted it, landing on the deck as if he'd done it plenty of times.

"I learned to jump from riding rodeo,'' he said with a flourish. He handed her the roses. "Thornless,'' he said.

She was too shocked to say anything.

"Cissy," he said, "I screwed up everything."

"Not everything," she replied. "What are you doing here? And how did you find me?"

"Jellyfish logged his trip properly, but he'd also told Hawk where he was going in case he needed him for another finder's mission. Hawk is not hard to get ahold of, and he seems to have a lot of information. I knew I could count on him," Tex said. "But that's really not important. I would have found you wherever you were, Cissy. We didn't end things right."

"Right?"

"I don't think so. I've taken a long time to think about it, and I think you should marry me."

"We are married." In her heart, Cissy had dreamed of hearing these words from Tex again.

"Married properly, forever, and in between."

"Are you serious?" she whispered, her heart beginning to race as she realized that he was here for the real deal, the true proposal she'd always dreamed of. She hugged the roses to her.

"Yes. We might be married," he agreed, "but if you wish to stay married under our deal of convenience, then I would like to put forth the idea that we still have one point left that we didn't cover. I never made love to you properly."

She stared at him. "Oh, yes, I think that is the one area where I can truthfully say that you did not let me down."

He grinned. "You make a man feel better, Cissy, when he's been an ass. However, I believe the point of agreement was that I make love to you under the stars. All night long. And I have not done that. I have not completely honored my part of the bargain.''

"Oh, I see," she murmured.

"However, in the interest of moving forward, what I would really like to do is start over. As much as I enjoyed our marriage of convenience, I've realized that is not all I want from you. Nor is it all I want to give to you." He dropped to one knee on the deck, sweeping his hat from his head and placing it over his heart with one hand. With the other, he reached to take her hand as she held the flowers, the stone paperweight and the doily. "Other admirers?" he asked. "Did I get here just in the nick of time?"

She shook her head. "No admirers."

"Yes, admirers," he said with a mock sigh. "However, I understand their pain, since you are the only woman in the world I could ever love."

Her heart leaped inside her. "Tex—"

"Now, I know you've worried about the trashy issue," he said, holding up his hand. "I know you don't think you're the right woman for me. Believe me when I tell you that I've watched Mimi torture Mason all these years. I've seen him understand too late how much he enjoyed her. I don't want you to get away from me, Cissy. I like your sense of humor and your spunk. I like that you don't let me win, except in bed. Actually, I even like the way you're always one step ahead of me, and how you let me stew in my own juice for the past two weeks. You have a lot of respect for yourself, Cissy, and it's very, very becoming."

She felt tears gather in her eyes. "You see me differently than I see myself."

"It's okay," he said. "I don't mind telling you every day what a wonderful woman you are, if you'll let me. Now, put down those nice trinkets from those poor slobs who recognize an amazing lady when they see one, and let me propose to you with all the romanticism that I can muster."

Laughing, she put the rock, doily and flowers down on a deck table.

"Cissy Kisserton Jefferson," Tex said, taking her hands in his, "please marry me. I know that having me as a husband will be a hardship on some days, but on others, it will be fun. It will be sexy. There'll be lots of stars and skinny-dipping and anything else I can do to bring a smile to your face, because that's all I want, is to make you smile. And make love to you as often as I am physically able. Yeah," he said, no grin in his eyes at all, "I love you. I have from the day I slid your Make My Day panties off of you in the barn. The day that really got made was mine. Marry me, and be Mrs. Jefferson, and be my better half, because as God knows too well, I'm only going to be a sad, confused, slightly odd half without you in my life."

Cissy moved into his arms, and they sat on the deck together, she in his lap, enjoying his arms around her as they felt the riverboat start up. She leaned against his shoulder. "Thank you," she told Tex, "thank you for making all my dreams come true. I can't wait to be the real Mrs. Tex Jefferson."

They kissed, and the riverboat began to pull away.

"Thank you for making all my dreams come true," he told her, when the kiss finally ended. "I thought I'd lost you forever."

"I love you," she said. "There is no man like you on earth."

"Yeah, well, guess what? I'm not going to be on earth. I'm going to be on water." He sat up, trying to glance over the rail's edge unsuccessfully. "I'm going to have to learn how to drive this damn bathtub."

She turned to stare at him. "Why?"

"Because I made an offer to Jellyfish a few hours ago. I mean, Hawk is good, but I had to let Jellyfish know he needed to delay the trip by an extra couple of minutes if he was going to accept my offer. I'm not a superhero, though I've foolishly tried to be to impress you in the past."

"You bought the riverboat?" Cissy couldn't believe what she was hearing.

"What else would I give for an engagement gift?"

She squealed, throwing her arms around his neck for a tight hug.

"I just want you to know," he said, laughing, "that I never promised you a rose garden. Well, maybe I did. But I'm only making promises these days that I can deliver on. I can give you everything—except a rose garden."

She kissed him enthusiastically. "I have everything I need, and all that I ever wanted, thanks to you."

"Well, not everything. I'm seeing the children as wedding attendants, and maybe your brother gives

you away, and Gran totes out oatmeal raisin cookies.''

"And your brothers? How do they fit into the
plan?''

"They're simply rowers on the riverboat. I like the
image of them slaving away with oars. It will be fun
to have the whole gathering together. Yours, mine,
ours. We can let Jellyfish string his lights again, like
he did for Hannah's and Ranger's wedding—''

The squeals were nearly sonic now. He couldn't
stop smiling. "And then, there's this," he said, pulling something from his pocket. "It's not made of
rope, but I'd like it to last until our golden anniversary. So it's gold.''

He slipped a gold ring on her finger that had an
oval aquamarine surrounded by diamonds. "The blue
is for your eyes and for the water," he told her. "Not
that anyone is ever going to say that the Mississippi
is blue. But you get the imagery.'' He kissed her hair
as she stared mistily at the ring. "We could go back
to the rope rings, but they're not really built to last.''

She smiled at him, her heart blossoming with happiness. "Cowboy, I like the way you think.''

He grinned. "Then I've finally done everything
right.''

Cissy melted back into his arms, and Tex smiled
to himself, his heart full of the knowledge that for
the first time in his life, he knew exactly what intimacy was.

And he was never living without it again.

Epilogue

The entire Jefferson family attended Cissy's and Tex's splendidly romantic wedding on the riverboat. The evening was alive with happiness and reminiscing. Frisco Joe and Annabelle were there with baby Emmie, who seemed much changed to Tex. Time wasn't standing still, he realized, despite the brothers' secret wishes that they themselves stay the same. Yet, they'd all wanted change of a sort. All Frisco Joe wanted was to make changes at the ranch, but then he'd married Annabelle—the change in his life had been him. Annabelle glowed with a new pregnancy, and Frisco Joe looked like the happiest man on the planet.

Except, maybe, for Laredo. All Laredo had wanted was to Do Something Big, and catching Katy Goodnight had been something big. Moving to North Carolina was another big thing, because Laredo had settled into Katy's world at Duke University with a smile on his face. He'd decided to attend college, something he'd never wanted to do before—and Tex suspected it was only partly to be near Katy as often as possible.

Ranger didn't have quite the same contentment on his face—he was euphoric, for a man who claimed all he wanted was to join the military and to stay footloose all his life. Ranger couldn't stay away from Hannah. Tex grinned as he saw Ranger tuck a hand along Hannah's back. Tex's big, tough brother wasn't so tough anymore—and yet, somehow he was more man than ever.

Delilah had come to the wedding escorted by Jerry, and all the Union Junction stylist women and their Lonely Hearts Salon sisters, even though Cissy was a one-time rival. Bygones were bygones, and as always, the ladies pitched in to make everything just right for the wedding.

Mimi arrived without her father but with Brian. Helga was sitting at home with the sheriff so that Mimi could get away for the wedding. Not that any of them were ready to say that Helga was growing on them—none of the brothers would want her for a mother-in-law—but she'd quickly offered to sheriff-sit and Mimi had been relieved. That had won Helga super-points in Tex's book.

Of course, that left Mason hanging around the punch bowl. Under the beautifully strung lights, it was clear Mason was trying to have a good time. Mason was good at hiding his feelings now, but Tex knew his brother too well. Mason had missed out on Mimi, and now he was playing the good friend to the hilt for Brian's sake—for all their sakes. Mason had gone over to peer at Tex's handiwork around Mimi's pond one afternoon. He'd stared at the cattails and the sweet william gardens and the water lilies, and when Tex had mentioned he was going to build a pier so that all the Jefferson and Cannady kids could jump in the pond, Mason had grunted and turned away.

But not before Tex had seen his brother's face go a little strained. Ah, no, Mason was not over his feelings for Mimi. Maybe one day he'd find happiness with a woman the way the other brothers had....

Tex beamed at his beautiful bride. Cissy was an angel in white, holding Jellyfish's arm as he walked her down the makeshift aisle. A minister from Union Junction stood by to unite Cissy and Tex, but Cissy halted, leaning down to kiss Gran, tears in their eyes as they enjoyed the heirloom moment. Tex knew that the bond between the siblings and Gran had only grown stronger since they'd returned, and though they'd miss Cissy, they also loved each other enough to let her find her own happiness. Cissy had held the family on her shoulders long enough.

Of course, he'd take her home often to see her beloved ''children.'' Oh, they couldn't sit still in their chairs, and they'd strewn rose petals every which way from Sunday, but they brought a sweet turmoil into his life that he enjoyed. He resolved to build that pier at Mimi's pond quickly, as soon as he and Cissy returned from their first foray up the river.

''Ready, Captain?'' Cissy asked with a smile as she approached his side.

''Ready, Captain,'' he replied. ''The question is, are you?''

''I've never been more ready.''

He nodded, and took her hand in his. ''I can honestly say that I would never have been ready without you.''

She smiled. ''I never thought I'd have a dream come true, Tex. But I did, and it's all because of you. Do you know that I never thought I'd say that to anyone?''

''I love you,'' he replied with a smile. ''You make

it so easy to love you in ways I never knew I could love someone.''

"Let the preacher-man marry you two already!" one of the brothers called. "Enough romancing!"

Tex and Cissy grinned at each other.

The romancing had just begun.

And after the vows were spoken and the reception was over, Tex and Cissy threw birdseed on the laughing guests as they left the riverboat, in a departure from tradition. Then it was just the two of them, alone together on the boat of Cissy's dreams.

"Hey, Mrs. Jefferson," Tex said. "Come let me investigate that garter."

Cissy laughed.

"Let me help you drop that gorgeous gown to the ground," he continued, reaching for her zipper as he kissed his bride's neck.

"Tex," Cissy said, feeling her body respond to his caress. "Whatever can you be thinking?"

"That I've one last promise to keep to my woman. I promised you the stars, and tonight, I'm going to make love to you while we count them together."

She smiled as he slipped her gown from her shoulders. "I plan on losing count so you'll have to keep loving me."

"Even if there were no stars in the sky, Cissy Jefferson, I would still be out here making love to you. Nothing could stop me. I've waited for you forever."

And then, together, they discovered that their love had certainly been worth the wait.

* * * * *

Don't miss Fannin's story coming in spring 2004 from American Romance! Turn the page for a sneak peek!

Chapter One

"What I'm saying is feel the romance, Princess," Fannin said. "Smell the breeze. Hear the sigh of the grass. Rejoice in the call of the wild. Entice that bull, Princess, please," he pleaded with his cow to the delight of his brothers.

"Could you turn it up, Romeo?" Archer asked. "I don't think all of Union Junction has heard you spout such poetry in all the years you've lived here."

"Do you have to do it this way?" Calhoun complained. "Can't you just be normal and use a syringe to get a calf in her?"

"Hey!" Fannin said with a frown. "I know it's not logical. But Princess is conceiving the natural way."

"Or no way at all," Navarro said. "I see no interest on the part of her suitor."

Indeed, Bloodthirsty Black, usually such a fire-bringer of hell and mortification upon hapless cowboys, appeared disinterested in his bride.

"Why don't you tell Bloodthirsty how it's done, Fannin?" Archer asked, gasping with smothered laughter. "After all, you're the expert with women."

Fannin grimaced as his three brothers slapped each other on the backs. "I sort of have a date Saturday night," he said, not totally lying.

"A date!" They all leaned forward from their posts on the fence. "Who's the unfortunate girl?"

Fannin turned away so they couldn't see his face. "I'm taking Helga to the movies. She wants to see a movie in Dallas. And I think it's time she got off the ranch for a few hours. You dopes haven't noticed, but Helga's homesick. She's lonely. So I'm taking her out."

"Helga!" They roared with laughter.

Navarro grinned. "Yeah, I'd like to go out with a battle-ax. That'd be my choice of female companionship," he said insincerely.

"That's not very nice," Fannin said with a frown. "She's been working hard taking care of us and the sheriff. You know, you ought to think about taking her out yourselves. Helga's not here just to put up with your majestic egos."

They stared at him.

"Did you see that pair of twins on Rosie Mayflower?" Fannin mimicked in a high voice. That was exactly how his brothers would talk—and did talk—about women.

"Now those are some twins," Archer agreed. "Navarro, does Rosie have any cousins in another county with the same genetic traits? There has to be some family relations she could introduce us to."

"Breasts aren't everything," Fannin pointed out.

"But they are something," Navarro said, "and they count big-time in my book."

"Anyway," Archer said, "you're not even talking to Princess right, Fannin. A woman doesn't want to be begged or pleaded with for sex. She wants to be told how it's going to be. She wants to be ravaged. Stormed and conquered. If she knows what the game is up front, then she's happy to play. No wonder you don't have any real dates."

"Well, it's true that early cavemen didn't have any trouble getting women," Fannin said. "They just dragged the girls off by the hair."

"No point in getting rough," Calhoun said. "All we're suggesting is that your way is too subtle to get a woman's attention. Notice we get the women, while you tend to get the sister with the good personality and the insurmountable chastity."

"Because I don't storm the gates," Fannin finished.

"Afraid he's right," Navarro said. "Never let a woman have the upper hand, most especially in the sack, or you'll wind up with a Helga running your world, like Mason. In other words, you'll end up whipped, when you should be putting your feet up after a long day, with a very attractive female ready to bring you a beer, serve you your supper in a comfy arm chair, and then put you to bed with a smile on her face."

"That's what I mean," Fannin said sadly to Princess. "My brothers are all so artificial. They think of only one thing. Don't worry about that stupid bull not wanting you," he told his favorite cow. "He's probably lost all his good genes throwing cowboys around."

"Princess is not a pet," Calhoun said sternly.

"She is to me. Besides, the best things take time," Fannin said briskly. "And the right moment. Magic."

"And I say you're going to be waiting a helluva long time, you and your Princess." Archer slapped his hat against his leg and hopped off the rail. "I got work to do."

His brothers murmured something similar, leaving Fannin alone with Princess and her lackluster lover.

"Hey," he said to the bull, "you're supposed to be the hottest thing on hooves. What's your problem? I had to haul you out here in a special trailer so you wouldn't do damage to yourself. Half the county said I was crazed to even let you near Princess. They said, do it the right way, but I said no, natural was better. And look at you over there. You couldn't care less. I believe you're only good for the ring, you old show pony."

Fannin sighed, his brothers' words eating at him. It was true he didn't date much. He didn't use the ruthless technique, which, he had to admit, did seem to drive the women wild for his brothers. Truthfully, he had some things in common with Bloodthirsty Black. And last year had seen enough settling down to suit all the Jefferson brothers. So he was in no hurry to auto-date.

Helga wasn't much of a date, though, he had to admit that.

"I *would* like a date," Fannin told Princess. "Unfortunately, I'd be better off ordering up a girl. I could say, okay, this is what I want, and I want her to do this, and not to do that, and I don't want any flack about it. Then my brothers would have to shut up. But how do I get that?''

Princess ignored him.

''My brothers say their blue-ribbon goal is sex in the morning, every morning, and it'd be a best-case scenario if they could relieve themselves without having to worry about the woman. Who cares if she climaxes? And please get out of the bed quickly and quietly. Vamoose!'' He sighed with frustration. ''They're such syringe types.''

The only time a woman had come to the ranch without designs on any of them had been an accident. Actually, it had been *women* who'd arrived, courtesy of an e-mail that his eldest brother, Mason, and their next-door-neighbor, Mimi, had sent to the wrong place. All hell had broken loose when the females from Lonely Hearts Station had arrived.

But so many good things had come out of that stray e-mail.

And even Helga had been a result of that. Mimi had called her friend, Julia Finehurst of the Honey-Do Agency, to send out a female, one that Mason couldn't fall in love with, even though Mimi knew she'd never have Mason. Mimi was just that way about keeping Mason pinned in a corner.

Helga had arrived, and Fannin could honestly say the square, stout German housekeeper kept all the brothers in line. Like a military sergeant. Mimi had played the prank of all pranks on Mason.

But Fannin wouldn't want to marry anyone like tricky Mimi.

Maybe his brothers were right. His technique had to go, or he was going to end up alone, with Mason and his other flatheaded brothers.

"Good night," he said to the bounty bull. "I doubt you'll get matters figured out, but I'll leave you here a while just in case. And you, Miss Princess, you just try to be a docile lass if he comes a'courting."

He headed up to the house and went into Mason's office. It was quiet in here, and felt faintly like his father was still somewhere nearby. After all these years, Fannin recognized the presence. He sat down at the computer and began to type an e-mail.

"This is so anonymous," he murmured. "I kind of like it." He began to state his needs. "Attractive, understanding, somewhat petite female." He typed happily. "For a big-hearted cowboy who needs a special date. She needs to have a good sense of humor, too."

It felt like he was looking for an artificial female. "That's my problem," he said. "I'm always worrying about being heavy-handed. My brothers would just fire this puppy off and never think twice about sounding like tree-dwellers."

Well, Tarzan he wasn't, but he wanted a Jane, at least for one night. A Jane he'd practically designed himself. "There are bigger sins on the planet than being a male chauvinist. Here goes nothing," he said, hitting the Send key.

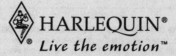

If you enjoyed what you just read,
then we've got an offer you can't resist!

Take 2 bestselling love stories FREE!

Plus get a FREE surprise gift!

Your opinion is important to us! Please take a few moments to share your thoughts with us about your experiences with Harlequin and Silhouette books. Your comments will be very useful in ensuring that we deliver books you love to read.
Please take a few minutes to complete the questionnaire, then send it to us at the address below.

Send your completed questionnaires to:
Harlequin/Silhouette Reader Survey, P.O. Box 9046, Buffalo, NY 14269-9046

1. As you may know, there are many different lines under the Harlequin and Silhouette brands. Each of the lines is listed below. Please check the box that most represents your reading habit for each line.

Line	Currently read this line	Do not read this line	Not sure if I read this line
Harlequin American Romance	❑	❑	❑
Harlequin Duets	❑	❑	❑
Harlequin Romance	❑	❑	❑
Harlequin Historicals	❑	❑	❑
Harlequin Superromance	❑	❑	❑
Harlequin Intrigue	❑	❑	❑
Harlequin Presents	❑	❑	❑
Harlequin Temptation	❑	❑	❑
Harlequin Blaze	❑	❑	❑
Silhouette Special Edition	❑	❑	❑
Silhouette Romance	❑	❑	❑
Silhouette Intimate Moments	❑	❑	❑
Silhouette Desire	❑	❑	❑

2. Which of the following best describes why you bought *this book?* One answer only, please.

the picture on the cover	❑	the title	❑
the author	❑	the line is one I read often	❑
part of a miniseries	❑	saw an ad in another book	❑
saw an ad in a magazine/newsletter	❑	a friend told me about it	❑
I borrowed/was given this book	❑	other: _____	❑

3. Where did you buy *this book?* One answer only, please.

at Barnes & Noble	❑	at a grocery store	❑
at Waldenbooks	❑	at a drugstore	❑
at Borders	❑	on eHarlequin.com Web site	❑
at another bookstore	❑	from another Web site	❑
at Wal-Mart	❑	Harlequin/Silhouette Reader	
at Target	❑	Service/through the mail	❑
at Kmart	❑	used books from anywhere	❑
at another department store or mass merchandiser	❑	I borrowed/was given this book	❑

4. On average, how many Harlequin and Silhouette books do you buy at one time?

I buy _____ books at one time	❑
I rarely buy a book	❑

MRQ403HAR-1A

5. How many times per month do you shop for any *Harlequin and/or Silhouette* books?
One answer only, please.

1 or more times a week	❏	a few times per year	❏
1 to 3 times per month	❏	less often than once a year	❏
1 to 2 times every 3 months	❏	never	❏

6. When you think of your ideal heroine, which *one* statement describes her the best?
One answer only, please.

She's a woman who is strong-willed	❏	She's a desirable woman	❏
She's a woman who is needed by others	❏	She's a powerful woman	❏
She's a woman who is taken care of	❏	She's a passionate woman	❏
She's an adventurous woman	❏	She's a sensitive woman	❏

7. The following statements describe types or genres of books that you may be
interested in reading. Pick *up to 2 types* of books that you are most interested in.

I like to read about truly romantic relationships	❏
I like to read stories that are sexy romances	❏
I like to read romantic comedies	❏
I like to read a romantic mystery/suspense	❏
I like to read about romantic adventures	❏
I like to read romance stories that involve family	❏
I like to read about a romance in times or places that I have never seen	❏
Other: _____	❏

*The following questions help us to group your answers with those readers who are
similar to you. Your answers will remain confidential.*

8. Please record your year of birth below.
19 _____

9. What is your marital status?
single ❏   married ❏   common-law ❏   widowed ❏
divorced/separated ❏

10. Do you have children 18 years of age or younger currently living at home?
yes ❏   no ❏

11. Which of the following best describes your employment status?
employed full-time or part-time ❏   homemaker ❏   student ❏
retired ❏   unemployed ❏

12. Do you have access to the Internet from either home or work?
yes ❏   no ❏

13. Have you ever visited eHarlequin.com?
yes ❏   no ❏

14. What state do you live in?
_____

15. Are you a member of Harlequin/Silhouette Reader Service?
yes ❏   Account # _____   no ❏   MRQ403HAR-1B

An offer you can't afford to refuse!

High-valued coupons for upcoming books

A sneak peek at Harlequin's newest line—Harlequin Flipside™

Send away for a hardcover by *New York Times* bestselling author Debbie Macomber

How can you get all this?

Buy four Harlequin or Silhouette books during October–December 2003, fill out the form below and send the form and four proofs of purchase (cash register receipts) to the address below.

HARLEQUIN®
Live the emotion™

Silhouette™
Where love comes alive™

Visit us at www.eHarlequin.com

Q42003